Rosie Sees the Light

Rosie Sees the Light

a novel

Pam, dear friend and enthusiastic supporter,

Enjoy Rosie's adventures!

Carol Fogel

Carol Fogel

For Mother

Chapter 1

Rosie saw the white light. Its stark brilliance blinded her. A whack to her shrunken chest forced the cold metal table into her back. She squinted into the whiteness and saw folks milling around, but no one she knew. So, she declined, *thank you very kindly*, to join them. *Is that Jesús?* He looked pale and peaked. Must be that bright light, not flattering to anyone, not even Him. He looked worried, too. *Hasta la vista, Jesús.*

She awoke in her own bed, but not in her own home.

She remembered.

How many months ago was it? Alex had stuffed her suitcase, telling her, in an oh-so cheerful strained voice, "Mom, think of this as going on a vacation." *Dios*, he must think her old and stupid to believe that line. How many people went on vacation to an old folks' home? Oh, excuse me, an assisted living facility?

For a time, the stroke left her without a voice. Now her vocal chords and brain worked in tandem, but she hadn't shared her healing with anyone. No one seemed to care, except for Alex. She knew he wanted to hear that she liked it at Shady Oaks, that her life was so much easier. But, most of all, he wanted her to say that he did the right thing. She couldn't lie to him, so she chose the kinder response—none at all.

Every day he arrived with "a few more new things you might need, Mom" and crammed them into her closet: dark polyester slacks and neutral tops, price tags dangling, no doubt his wife Judith's idea of an aging woman's fashion statement. Rosie kept on wearing her washed out denims and bespangled Snoopy Christmas sweater most days to remind herself that *every day's a present*, she wanted to tell anyone who asked, but no one did.

In Alex's quest to help her "settle in," he cluttered her small room with knick-knacks brought from her home: multiple statues of the Virgin Mother and Jesús, a lopsided vase—her first project in ceramics class years back, several subsequent attempts at whimsical dogs, and a large black crow—her final project and her best. She had made it for Alex's thirteenth birthday, and it had become their private joke, a clay-fired admonishment to him when he tested her patience. Straighten up and fly right!

How could Alex think new clothing and a bunch of old figurines would make her accept this place?

Despite the passage of time, Rosie's mind kept returning to and replaying the film of what she had come to title "The White Light Wakeup Call." She heard the message loud and clear. You got away this time. But next time…. And that message had been delivered by none other than Jesús Himself. But what was she to do about His warning? She puzzled and prayed until the answer came. *What I need is one last great adventure.* First and last great adventure, actually, because her life could be best described as circumspect and careful, all 73 years of it.

"I'm entering my colorful period," she told the youthful department store personal shopper, who scouted out possibilities. A week later, Rosie returned and finalized her choices. She paid in cash. Like a co-conspirator, the young woman stuffed the items into one bag. Rosie didn't want any comments or questions from the Shady Oaks van driver or anyone else about the volume of her purchases.

Back in her room after her excursion to the mall, she wheeled a black suitcase from the far corner of her closet and hefted it atop her bed. She unfurled the garments from the shopping bag and admired them: slacks in bright magenta, purple and turquoise; matching floral blouses and sweaters; new underwear with patterns of spring blossoms; and a bathing suit. Rosie smiled at its yellow hibiscus flowers. No old lady black bathing suit with a skirt. *They'll see me coming.* After she refolded each item and stacked them all in her suitcase, Rosie gave a benedictory pat to the pile. She slipped the closed case back into her closet and shut the door.

That night, with a compliant grin directed at her bedtime attendant, Rosie cupped the offered pills in her palm, drank deeply of the water, and swallowed with a gulp. Alone at last, she crept into the bathroom, cast the medications into the bowl, and flushed. *Sleep well, dear toilet.* Rosie hid beneath her comforter and shone her flashlight on her notebook. *My Last Adventure begins*, she wrote.

Escape was easy. She knew from watching the attendants who smoked. *What kind of idiots still smoked?* Just sneak out the rear door that didn't have an alarm, despite its *Alarm Will Sound* warning sign. Like much of life, there were posted signs, and there was the truth. Rosie pushed the door into the silent night and was gone.

Later, when questioned, the night shift personnel would all attest that their midnight bed check had shown Rosie asleep in her bed. She'd been there all right, fully clothed in her many-hued ensemble, awake with eyes shut, poised to slip minutes later into the world once more.

Peaceful darkness enveloped Rosie. She wheeled her suitcase behind and hummed the tune of O*n the Wings of an Angel.* In front of Harold's Diner, she found a waiting cab. *Thank you, dear Mary Mother of God.* From the back seat, she fingered the silver crucifix she never removed from around her neck and sent another gracias over the driver's dark and curly head.

"To the bus station, please," she said.

Chapter 2

The street outside the downtown bus station smelled of urine. She entered the building and headed in a myopic beeline for the ladies' restroom, pulling the suitcase in her wake. Suddenly the piece of luggage jolted, and she turned to see why. A uniformed officer with dark eyes glared down at her. *Does he recognize me? Have they reported me missing already?* She saw her carry-on jammed against his legs and resting on a booted foot.

"I'm so sorry, officer." She yanked her suitcase, dragging it across his other shoe. "Sorry again."

"No problem, ma'am. Just watch out for children and small animals."

When Rosie pulled open the heavy ladies' room door, sharp antiseptic smells burned her nose. In a stall, she squatted over the seat. Before she exited, she removed several twenties from her bra, patted her chest and heard the comforting crinkle of more bills. She stretched her sweater down over her front. Never been a D cup, until now. She didn't want to attract the wrong kind of attention.

Her passport was nine years old. She looked good in it, but remembered how she had never liked that photo, thought it made her look old. Now, she just hoped she was recognizable as the woman in the photo. The ticket seller flipped his eyes up at her, down at her passport, and shoved it back across the counter along with a ticket.

She followed a crowd of travelers to the bus. Like her, a few people trailed wheeled suitcases behind them, but most carried older models by handles, and some wrestled along cardboard boxes. The bus driver flung the cases and parcels into the undercarriage, without regard to their contents. No one protested. Rosie took what she decided was a safe seat, beside a young mother with a baby. Although she would have preferred a window, Rosie didn't want to take the chance of a strange man sitting next to her.

"Hello," Rosie said.

"Hello," the woman replied in Spanish-accented English. She kept her eyes on her baby as she gently rocked the infant.

"How old is your baby...boy or girl?"

"Boy. He is six weeks."

"What is his name?"

"Juan."

Most of Rosie's friends had grandchildren by now. Alex would be a good father, but he and Judith had never mentioned children.

The bus engine rumbled to life, and the coach swung out of the station onto the city streets. From her seat, Rosie saw shapes huddled under blankets in dark doorways. *Do their families know where they are? God, be with them.* Her eyes filled. She dabbed the tears and sat up straight. Enough of this. *I'm on my way.*

The bus pulled onto the freeway and accelerated. The vibration of the motor and the sway of the carriage carried her away to sleep.

She sensed movement next to her and struggled to wake up. Her seat companion's body shook.

"Juan will not nurse," the young woman said, tilting her head toward her breasts. Tears dripped down her face onto the baby.

"Is he sick?"

"Yes."

Rosie reached out to touch the baby's forehead. She felt heat, and saw that his round face burned a furious red. "We must cool him down, and get him to drink some fluids." She dug a handkerchief and bottle of water from her satchel and soaked the handkerchief with water. The baby squirmed when she placed the wet cloth on his head.

Rosie forgot her caution with strangers, stood up, and addressed the entire bus in a loud voice. "Does anyone have any juice and a baby bottle? We have a sick baby here."

Hours later, the bus cruised along the freeway as Juan slept on Rosie's lap. The young mother had lost her fight to stay awake, and her head slumped against Rosie's shoulder. Although Juan still felt warm, he wasn't as feverish as he had been. His round belly was full of replenishing juices, but he was still very sick. He needed medical attention, as soon as they got across the border. She stroked his soft legs. Despite the hour, Rosie felt alert and alive.

Throughout the night people edged into the aisle and leaned over her to check on the infant. One man, dressed in shabby clothing and smelling like he'd needed a bath for a long time, held out some coins in his soiled hand. "For the little one," he said. She wouldn't have sat next to him, that's for sure.

"Thank you, sir, but I have money for his care," Rosie said.

He flushed and turned away.

She reached out and touched his arm. "Señor, if you can spare a few pesos, it would be most helpful."

He gave her several coins and bowed his head to her.

"Gracias, señor." Rosie said.

"De nada, señora," he replied.

The bus slowed and stopped. Rosie's arms ached from holding Juan, and she straightened in her seat again. Bright lights illuminated the border crossing. Her seatmate smiled and reached for the baby, his limp body offering little response. He was too quiet, not even a whimper.

The uniformed Mexican immigration officer mounted the steps and peered into the bus lit by dim overhead lights. He marched down the aisle. Like the passengers around her, her seat companion kept her eyes down and her passport held high. Rosie did the same. The official strode to the back of the bus and returned to the front. He slapped the driver's shoulder and departed. Conversations buzzed. How often did someone try to sneak into Mexico? By his perfunctory search, Rosie guessed not often.

When the bus rolled past the "Welcome to Mexico" sign, she made the sign of the cross, dug out her notebook, and wrote: *My name is Rosaria.*

Memories of the distant past flashed, clearer than yesterday's events. She saw her mother shaking wet sheets into the wind, holding them up to the wash line, pushing wooden clothes pins into place. Mamá always appeared so pleased with herself as she gave each wet piece a final smoothing stroke with her hand.

When Rosaria was ten, her parents immigrated to California, settling in the San Gabriel Valley near Los Angeles among others like themselves. Rosaria learned English in school and borrowed piles of books from the library. "You are smart, Rosaria. You can go to college," her teachers told her. Instead, one month after her high school graduation, she walked down the parish aisle into marriage, an expectation of her community. Another expectation—motherhood—proved more difficult. After more than six years, their son was born.

Longino had been a good husband and the proudest father. "How's my little man?" was each evening's greeting to baby Alejandro.

She expected their small life to unfold just like the lives around them. It didn't. Her husband's lingering cough grew into a malignant death sentence. Before Alejandro learned to say "Daddy," Rosaria sat with her toddler son in church for Longino's funeral mass.

Later, a few years after the boy did learn to talk, he told her, "No more Alejandro, Mom. My name is Alex." As Alex embraced the life of an American boy, Rosaria tried to keep up. She stopped being Rosaria. She became Rosie.

She snapped back to the present. Her help was needed, here and now. She turned to the young woman. "My name is… Rosaria." The softened r's rolled off her tongue.

"I am María."

"Please let me help you, María."

The bus brakes hissed, and the vehicle pulled to a stop. Passengers gathered their possessions to exit. Rosaria stood up. "Please. Does anyone know where we can find a doctor for our baby?"

A mother pulled two toddlers up to Rosaria's seat. "There is one doctor here. I will take you to him," she said. A tattooed young man insisted on wheeling Rosaria's suitcase and toting María's bag. He loped along, head jerking to the music from his ear buds. In another life—yesterday—Rosaria would have refused his help. She would have thought he meant to steal from her. A sick baby brought out the best in people, including her. They paraded through the quiet town center and stopped at a battered metal door. A wooden sign above the door flapped in the breeze: *El Médico de Medicina General*.

After no response to their persistent knocking, the young man picked up a fist-sized rock and pounded. Now Rosaria understood the origins of the many dents in the door.

The only doctor in town was not happy to see them at five in the morning. He yanked at his hair and rubbed his eyes with long fingers, his fingernails jagged, with dirt caught beneath.

"Put him over there." The doctor gestured to a cracked leather examination table. Rosaria patted María's back and guided her toward the table. Rosaria watched the doctor rinse his hands at the sink. She saw no soap.

"Doctor, please wash your hands with soap," Rosaria said. "And is that water hot?"

"Hot enough." He reached within a cabinet and brought out a sliver of dried-up soap.

She saw a box of surgical gloves next to the sink and looked from the doctor to the gloves. He shrugged, pulled a pair from the box, and yanked and snapped them over his hands.

Juan offered feeble cries at the doctor's prodding. The doctor's brow furrowed after he read the thermometer he removed from the baby's ear. María stood with her hands tightly clasped, eyes closed, whispering to an unseen deity. Rosaria kept her eyes on the doctor. He went to a closet and returned with a hypodermic needle.

"What's wrong with him?" Rosaria asked.

"This baby needs an antibiotic," he replied as he approached the baby.

"Wait. I asked you what's wrong with him."

"All you need to know is that he's very sick."

"I need to know exactly what's wrong before you start shooting antibiotics into this baby."

"And where did you get your medical degree, old woman?"

"I've seen so many doctors in my day that I could have several degrees."

"I can't give you a diagnosis until I do blood and stool tests."

"I want to take him to a hospital…now."

"You're in it."

The baby's small chest shrank with each breath.

"You need to explain what you're doing, and why, before you do anything."

"The antibiotic will start fighting whatever infection he has." His mouth twisted. "And, if it's acceptable to you, of course, I'll hook him up to an IV. Based on your vast medical experience, I'm sure you already know he needs that."

He went to the cupboard and returned with the supplies. As he passed María, he leaned close and whispered something to her that Rosaria could not hear.

"When you are finished, we will need some breakfast," Rosaria said.

"There's a café down the street. I don't provide room service," the doctor replied.

Rosaria turned her back and dug a fist full of bills out of her clothing. She thrust it toward him. "We're not leaving Juan. This is for the baby's treatment and for food for us. When he recovers, I will pay you more. María and I will need beds, too…in this room, and the use of a bathroom."

"That all?"

"For now," Rosaria said. "I'll let you know if we need anything else."

His body stiffened. He straightened to his full height and strode from the room.

Rosaria turned to María, who stood like a Madonna statue over her child. Rosaria put her arm around her.

"You are brave, Señora Rosaria."

"María, what did the doctor say to you?"

"He said that if I do not have money, not to worry. He will treat my baby if I am…nice to him," she replied.

"Over my dead body!" Rosaria made a quick sign of the cross in swooping gestures.

María gazed down at her small baby on the large table. His eyes were shut, and his chest rose and fell in the rhythms of sleep. "I am so worried."

Rosaria embraced her, and María sagged. "Juan will be fine, María. And I will not let that man touch you. Let's keep Juan cool. Wet some cloths and wipe his face."

With María's attention again on Juan, Rosaria drifted over to the doctor's cabinet. On the top shelf, she found a black zippered case. The doctor's surgical instruments. She took out one of the scalpels and tested its sharpness on the outside of the case. The blade left a deep slash in the darkened leather.

As soon as the cots were dragged into the room by a sour young woman, María pushed her cot up next to the examining table and extended one hand to cover Juan's tiny fist. Rosaria suddenly felt exhausted. She pulled her cot across the room until it was tight against the interior door. When the doctor returned, she needed to be awake. As she shifted in her cot, she sneezed and pulled the scratchy blanket over her head.

In her right hand, she gripped the doctor's knife.

Chapter 3

The phone roused him early. He reached for his bedside phone and knocked over a living room lamp. He had forgotten where he spent the night. He heard Judith's voice from the bedroom.

She brought the phone to him.

"Alex, this is Anna at Shady Oaks," he heard.

"Is my mom okay?"

"I don't want to alarm you, but she seems to be missing."

"What?"

"When she didn't show up for breakfast, an aide checked her room. She wasn't there. We've searched all over our facility. She's not here."

"How could this happen?" he asked, a question to which he knew there could be no satisfactory answer. "I'll be right over."

"Now what?" Judith asked.

"Mom's gone."

"I'm sorry, Alex. But it's probably for the best. Did she die during the night?"

"Not dead. Disappeared. They can't find her."

"She was hardly able to walk." Alex noted her use of the past tense.

As he drove, Alex willed himself to slow down. His mind drifted. He was back in the sadness of the day he dropped her off at Shady Oaks. No one told him how hard it would be. After he left her, Alex had slammed the truck door, sat down hard, and rested his head against the steering wheel. He blinked to clear his vision. *Stop it! Get hold of yourself!* Mom hadn't cried, so what was wrong with him? He remembered babbling on and on to her about how this place is so nice, Mom. She had nodded, more in resignation than in confirmation, he thought. Yeah, right. In reality, it was easier for him. Gone would be the multiple calls to her each day, holding his breath until she got to the phone. With her in that place, he could relax. She'd adjust. Besides, her own doctor said she needed to be cared for, that she was just one fall away from tragedy.

The brick facility, with not one oak tree in sight despite its name, stood tall and accusing against the early morning sky. The place had security alarms on the doors, not so much for people trying to get in, as for residents trying to get out, he had figured out. And why did they call them residents? A euphemism for what they really were—old people with nowhere else to go.

Ah, yes, euphemism, one of Mom's high-scoring Scrabble words. When he was a little boy, she tricked him into learning new words. When he told her he was thirsty, she replied, "You're dehydrated, are you?" When he spit on the sidewalk—a new skill he learned on the playground—she said, "Please do not expectorate on the pavement." Then, when they played one of their endless games of Scrabble, she would throw in one of her *grande* words, as she called them.

His mind was all over the place.

One person was happy with his mother's new living arrangement—Judith. What's with a woman who must be called Judith? Why not Judy? Jude? He'd tried to give her what he thought were pet names, indications of affection, but she corrected him.

"Please call me Judith," she said, in a tone that left him feeling like he did when the elementary teachers scolded him for one of his many infractions.

"Alex, you're a spirited boy...a boy with some spunk to him," his mother told him when he got in trouble at school. She had a knack for making him feel better, and her hugs sealed their deal. Judith wasn't much of a hugger. Why had that popped into his head? *I'm trying to find someone to be angry at, someone to blame.*

His mother's stroke had left her lopsided, with an odd, lurching gait. Her continued inability to speak puzzled her doctors. She refused to even attempt to form words. Instead, she glared at her speech therapist with what Alex recognized as her evil eye look. When his teenage mischief had threatened to escalate, that same look had whipped him into shape.

No walker for her. Instead, Mom used an old wooden staff that she brought back from Mexico when her mother died. When he met her plane, she emerged hefting the carved pole, which nearly matched her height. Only his mother could have convinced the crew to stow it onboard. After her stroke, she held the pole in a two-handed grip, and lumbered along, more like a determined mountain hiker than the failing old lady she had become. At least she allowed him to saw off the bottom to a more manageable height. He had to admit her balance was improving; she no longer leaned into her cane. He saw her posture returning and her steps accelerating. *Knowing Mom, she's probably set herself a goal.* All her life she had set an example of self-improvement, taking evening classes and writing her accomplishments in a notebook she carried in her pocket. Where was that notebook now?

Her silence had disquieted him. He decided pride prevented her from trying to form words. Her first attempts to communicate were humiliating, and she seemed to have given up. He missed her voice and pleaded with her to talk. He brought her the old Scrabble board, but she smiled up at him, shook her head, and pushed the game away. He needed her scolding him for not wearing a jacket, for needing a haircut, for working too many hours. I'm a grown man, but I still need my mom. *What if I never hear her voice again?*

Without conscious navigating, Alex found himself pulling into the Shady Oaks' parking lot. He raced from the car and flung open the door to the usual quiet of the place. A few old people shuffled along a corridor, while others sat waiting in the lobby for new faces to enter. He had expected to arrive and find frenetic activity—uniformed aides carrying walkie-talkies, and scurrying along the hallways and flinging open storage closets, but all was still.

Alex sprinted to his mother's room. As soon as he entered, he saw her form beneath the blankets. He gently lifted the covers as he exhaled in relief. "Rise and shine, Mom," he said.

Large rolls of neutral hued clothing occupied the center of her bed, price tags peeking out here and there. On her pillow, the ceramic crow reclined, its golden eyes flashing the refection of the overhead fluorescent light.

Alex's mind couldn't register what he was seeing. During his adolescent years, this same crow had occupied a central place on his bureau, its yellow eyes watching him—or so he imagined—and keeping him awake. Ultimately, he discovered that if he tumbled from his bed onto his knees and offered up a nighttime prayer for protection, sweet slumber came to him. A little healthy fear went a long way. He had decided he didn't want to make that bird, God, or his mom unhappy.

And soon after the bird's arrival, he and his mother created a leave-taking routine. She pushed back his dark bangs and pulled his shirt collar into satisfactory smoothness.

"Straighten up, and fly right," she said each day. He flung on his backpack, flapped his spindly arms, and squawked his best crow goodbye.

What was Mom saying to him today?

Then he remembered more: his teenage midnight adventures, covered up by the same ruse. He tried his mother's window, thinking she might have used his favored escape route. The window was sealed and didn't open. She had left another way.

He felt a hand on his shoulder and jumped.

"Alex, she'll turn up. She couldn't have gotten far," Anna said. "No need to involve the police yet."

"You have no idea what my mother is capable of. I'm calling the police."

Chapter 4

Something bumped Rosaria's cot. Morning smells of frying tortillas drifted in through the crack in the wooden door. *Mamá?* Her eyes shot open. Someone on the other side of the door was pushing, and it wasn't Mamá. Just as she'd planned, her cot blocked the entry. Rosaria stretched her legs down and her arms up. The scalpel flashed in her right hand.

"Let me in."

"Okay, okay," Rosaria replied. She rolled to her side, crawled like a crab off the low cot to the floor, and struggled to stand up. At that moment she remembered the repartee she and little Alex had shared when they traveled, "If I ever get home in my own little bed, I'm never leaving again." It was their private communication for: *There's no place like home.* At this moment, Rosaria yearned for her own little bed, but where did that exist for her anymore? She stood up taller. *I'm on my way home. Yes, I am.* She tucked the knife beneath the pillow and slid the cot away from the door. She smoothed down her fly-away hair and pulled the door open.

"What's the idea of blocking the door?" the doctor said. He pushed his way in.

"Didn't want to fall out of bed, so I pushed my cot against the door." She stepped aside and watched him walk past her to the baby and María. María slept next to her child in the hospital bed. The doctor extended his right hand.

"Don't touch her," Rosaria said in a low voice.

He jerked back his hand. "Relax, old woman. I just want to check on the boy."

He went around the bed to the baby's side. He felt the child's forehead, then inserted the thermometer. Juan's eyes opened and he squealed in protest. The flattening IV bag held only another inch of fluid. Rosaria pointed at it.

"Yes, yes, I see it," he said.

Rosaria froze, watching him as he strode to the cabinet and opened its door. She could see the scuffed black medical bag on its shelf. How often was he called upon to do surgery? She offered up a prayer for good health in the village, at least for the next few days, until they left. He reached into the cabinet to open the small refrigerator within and retrieved a full IV bag. Rosaria blew out an exhale of relief when he closed the cupboard door.

"What's Juan's temperature?" she asked.

"Still too high," he replied.

She wanted to know the precise number, but weighed the wisdom of pressing him. María gripped Rosaria's hand and held on.

"Juan is improving, isn't he?" Rosaria said.

The doctor shrugged. "A little, yes."

"We're hungry," Rosaria said.

"I told you before, there's a café across the street," he said.

"María doesn't want to leave her baby."

"Go and bring back some food for her."

María's cold hand squeezed Rosaria's harder.

"I don't think that will work for us," Rosaria said. She turned from him and reached with her free hand inside her shirt. "Here's some money. Send someone to bring us breakfast."

He snatched the money from her hand and pulled the door shut with a bang.

"The doctor, he is a bad man," María said. "I am sorry to say this, but you are old, and he is a strong man,"

"I have a secret weapon," Rosaria said.

The days passed with a stultifying sameness, but Rosaria never relaxed her vigilance. A few patients came to the doctor's door. She could hear him conversing with them in the adjoining room. She peered out to see them leaving with bottles of pills. Her prayers were answered; none needed his surgical skills. Nights she dropped onto her cot against the door and slept with comforting dreams of her mother and father. She was a child again, playing in the sand, the sun warming her face so real that she was startled to wake in a dark room. Upon awakening her parents stayed with her. She felt their benign presence so strongly that when she observed the rotating ceiling fan, she was surprised she did not see them floating above her.

Juan improved each day. The doctor was in and out of their room to tend to the baby. He seemed to have forgotten

María's presence, and responded to Rosaria's questions, but volunteered nothing.

The day came when the baby's temperature was normal, his color had returned to its healthy pink, and he began to nurse again. One more night, this night, and they could leave.

Rise and shine! Her mother's laughing voice called down the hall to Rosaria's bedroom. *Rise and shine, Rosaria!* A rooster crowed in affirmation. Rosaria opened her eyes to the blackness surrounding her. The cot shifted as she rolled to her side. A dream, it had just been a dream. No, she heard the rooster's deep-throated squawk again. Heavy footsteps pounded down the hall toward her door. She sat up on the cot, braced her feet on the floor, and leaned against the door, only to feel her feet sliding helplessly. The door swung open and her bed skidded across the floor. Rosaria tumbled off and slipped on the smooth floor as she tried to stand.

She smelled the doctor before she could see him, strong sweat and stronger alcohol.

"No way you're leaving here without me getting…" His massive hands grabbed the door frame for balance.

Rosaria swept her hand under her pillow and leaped at the doctor with the scalpel held high. She thrust forward with her full body behind the blow. The scalpel cut through the back of his left hand and pinned it to the door frame. His eyes rolled back, and he lost consciousness. As he slumped, the knife tore through his hand and released him.

Rosaria's stomach roiled. She fought to stay standing.

"Rosaria, Rosaria, we must go! Now!"

Her feet slipped in his blood. Somehow they made it outside. María carried the baby and gripped Rosaria's hand, pulling her along.

"Keep moving, Rosaria!"

Chapter 5

The police hadn't been much help, telling him he couldn't file an official report until his mother had been missing 24 hours. They placated him by doing exactly what he'd done, examined her room. They pointed to her cane propped against the wall, telling him she was probably still in the building, that they'd conduct a search.

When they left, they said, sure-sure, they'd drive around the neighborhood, too.

With his mind churning—all questions—no answers, Alex accelerated down the street toward home. He was late getting back…real late, and he hoped Judith wasn't angry. Sometimes she got that way when he didn't get home right on the dot. But tonight, each time he decided to give up, he would find himself turning his car onto another side street. His eyes swept both sidewalks, hoping to see his mother lumbering along. One street led to another, until he had to admit he was so far from Shady Oaks that his mom couldn't have possibly walked so far.

Alex opened his front door to warm cooking smells and cold silence. I should've called. Judith served dinner at seven, precisely. She was dependable. He liked that about her. By the time he had met her, he'd had enough of wild-child girls and wanted a stable, grownup woman.

He remembered her the first night he spotted her on a barstool, curvy figure in black with her long brown hair swept back with a sparkling clip. She watched the piano player plunk out *My Way,* her well-formed leg swinging to the beat. Alex was accustomed to instant access to females: a glance, a smile, and that did it. But there she sat, brunette and aloof, unaware of him. He slid toward her, until his elbow almost touched hers, and leaned in with his best grin. She kept her eyes on the performer.

"Come here often?" he asked.

She turned her head in his direction. "If I did, you'd already know, wouldn't you?" She pivoted away.

He was dismissed. He moved away from her.

Despite his best efforts not to, he thought about her, a lot. There she sat the next Friday night. Same piano player, different song, and her. He tried to look anywhere but at her, but his eyes drifted her way every few minutes. Not even that great looking, curves on the way to future fatty. Still, his eyes swept over the crowd and back to her, in a disturbing repetition he was helpless to stop. By the fourth Friday night, Alex pushed his way into the bar, crazy with the anticipation of her.

Their courtship—what a quaint word that was—challenged him. He dodged and darted like a fighter in the ring, not quite sure whether he was scoring points, but never retreating to his corner. His mother watched from the sidelines.

He was relieved that his two women shared a love of cooking. Judith gave his mom what she called "the latest" recipes she cut out of magazines. His mom took them, offering polite thanks. Later he saw them in her trash when he dumped it for her. He didn't tell Judith.

His mother's recipes were her legacy, kept in a faded cardboard box, handwritten on yellowing recipe cards. Each recipe's lifespan was carbon dated by its smears of ingredients. The more smears, the more often he had devoured it: pork in escabeche sauce, sopapilla, cheesecake pie. When his mom cooked for him and Judith, she offered Judith her recipes, but Judith wasn't interested in making any of Mom's Mexican dishes. Judith wanted to cook Mediterranean cuisine, she told Rosie. Alex saw the puzzled glance his mom shot at Judith. Thankfully, Judith didn't notice.

Their first Thanksgiving as a married couple had turned into an epicurean cook-off, each woman pushing her special dish his way, encouraging him to have a second helping of hers. To keep them both happy, he ate every food he was offered, until he groaned and staggered from the table to the sofa. Both women grinned, each certain she had won, that he had preferred her cooking. Although he never voiced it, any of his mom's dishes beat Judith's chicken souvlaki with fennel salad any day. He would forever favor the Mexican cuisine of his mother, but he knew to keep quiet. If each woman thought she was the winner, there were no losers. Alex thought he'd been clever to figure this out for himself. Who said women were hard to understand? These two were transparent. Except now, he wasn't so sure about his mom.

He couldn't fathom her leaving him behind to worry, without a word of explanation. *Who was this woman who walked out of Shady Oaks into the night?*

Until her recent health reversals, Rosie took classes at adult education, declining the senior center classes because "they were for old people." She delighted in the vitality of people decades younger. She'd pull out her notebook and read to him. "Listen to what this young guy said today."

Judith preferred the solitude of a book or television. When they married, she was quick to put in her notice at work. He agreed because her clerical job in an office cubicle had seemed to him like solitary confinement. As a contractor, he got to be outdoors, supervising the building of homes. Judith could keep his business records. She wasn't ready to have kids yet, she told him; and he didn't push her about it.

Mom will be a terrific grandma. A clutch of fear gripped him. *Mom, where are you?*

"Sorry I'm late," he said. He cocked his head, a boyhood gesture of mercy. He realized, too late, that a stop at Pete's Petals might have smoothed his way. He pictured himself behind a profusion of flowers, thrusting them toward Judith. It had worked before. He found her in the den, her latest romance novel shielding her face.

"Did they find her?"

"The police came, searched around the place, but they

won't do anything more until tomorrow. I've been driving around looking for her. But nothing."

"Your dinner's in the oven." She returned to her book.

He retrieved his foil wrapped dinner plate from the oven, flicked off the harsh overhead fluorescent light, and sat down to eat in the dim light from the stove.

"Of course! That's where she is!" Alex said out loud, dropping his fork.

Alex jammed his truck into gear and roared toward his childhood home.

The interior living room lights flowed out and colored the nighttime lawn a muted gold. From his truck at the curb, Alex could see the family within—two adults and a young boy—all moving around in front of a big-screen television. A video game flashed on the television screen. His knock was answered by the out-of-breath dad.

"Sorry to bother you. I'm Alex Rodriquez. This used to be my mother's house."

The man in the doorway extended his hand. "I'm Tom Matthews."

"I'm looking for my mother. I had this crazy idea that she might have come here."

"Hey, Grace, when's the last time Rosie was over?"

"Mom's been here?" Alex asked.

A slender woman appeared in the doorway. "She was here yesterday. She comes over about once a week, sometimes more often if something interesting is blooming in her garden, as she likes to call it." She smiled as she spoke.

"She spoke to you?"

"Oh, her speech was a little slow, but you know your mom; she's never at a loss for words."

Alex blinked. "I'm sorry she was over here bothering you."

"She isn't a bother, she's a sweet lady. She just wants to check out the back yard and enjoy the garden for a bit. Always checks out the flood channel out back, too, and tells us how much water's flowing. Actually, she's a great help. She knows her plants. Showed me how to trim the rose bushes. I've learned a lot from her. In August, she brought us her apple dessert recipes because she knew the apple tree was full. What's going on?"

"Mom left her senior residence, without a word to anyone."

"Oh, no!" Grace said. "What can we do?"

"Here's my business card. Please call me right away if she comes over."

"I'm sure she's fine. She'll turn up. She's quite a lady."

Chapter 6

A rooster crowed, and this one had his internal clock set right. Rosaria stretched, feeling new aches in old places. Just as the pain of a cramp dug into her right leg, she rolled to the left, and saw a Gila monster scratching the dirt. He extended his head and spit out his tongue. She scrambled backward, her soreness forgotten, flinging dirt with her feet. Rosaria pushed herself to her feet, grunting with the effort. One rooster and one Gila monster had accomplished what modern medicine couldn't. *Do I still have my pills?* She patted her pocket and heard the reassuring rattle of the bottles. Her mouth felt dry. Twists of worry tightened in her stomach.

"Where am I?" she said aloud and was startled by the gravely sound of her voice.

A pink morning mist spread over the low desert brush, and the rising sun added pale yellow to the morning palette. Rosaria brushed the desert dust off her long skirt and shook out her shawl. Where are María and Juan? She stared off into the brightening horizon. Low cactus and scrub growth dotted the landscape. No roads, no paths that she could see. The warming wind swirled puffs of dirt into her legs.

She remembered María's arm around her waist, pulling

her along as Rosaria's feet skidded over the rough terrain. How long had they run? How far away had they gotten? When Rosaria's breath had given out, and her feet refused to lift, María had lowered her to the ground. María had tucked Juan beneath her clothing and knelt over Rosaria. *Did she say anything to me? I can't remember.*

Rosaria's eye caught a nearby pile of rocks, too neatly stacked to be an accident. A piece of cloth fluttered in the breeze, held beneath the top stone. She moved closer. A piece of María's skirt. Rosaria pulled out the fabric and clasped it to her chest. *Oh, God, no. Am I standing on top of María's grave?* No hint of the earth being dug up, only smaller stones arranged on the ground. As she studied them, words emerged from the rock pattern: *Stay here! I will come back!* The extra effort to add exclamation marks comforted Rosaria. She kicked at the stones until the words disappeared but left the stack intact. María would need that to locate her.

Shade, she needed shade. She stripped off her blouse and removed her cotton bra and undershirt, and returned the blouse to her bare body. She put the bra over her head, with the cups over her ears, and the fastening under her chin. Finally, she draped the sleeveless undershirt over her head, positioning the two arm holes at her eyes. But even inside her clothing tent, she felt the sun burning through.

Rosaria walked in a widening circle, turning back at intervals to see the pile of rocks. When they were about to disappear into the far horizon, she found a slope leading to a dry river bed. As she stood on its edge, the bank gave way, and her feet slid out from under her. She sat down, hard, and skidded until a large stone halted and twisted her body. A sharp pain sliced her ribcage. She rolled to her side and pulled up her blouse. A dark bruise discolored her mid-section. Rosaria struggled to an upright position and willed herself to take shallow breaths.

Within the dry bed, an outcropping had been gouged by water during a rain-fed surge. She pushed herself underneath it, her head almost touching and leaned back against the bank. *I hope I didn't stir up my hemorrhoids.* She shook her head at that silly thought. Hemorrhoids were the least of her problems. *How about, hope I don't die out here?*

Quiet, broken by occasional gusts of wind, lulled Rosaria. Her chin drifted down to her chest, and her eyes shut. Sometime later, voices carried by the winds roused her. She struggled to stand, hit her head, and an avalanche of grit and pebbles cascaded over her. The voices grew closer.

"¡La loca está muerta!" reached her ears. She recognized the doctor's voice and froze. Another, more distant male voice yelled back. Danger whispered to her on the wind. *The crazy lady is dead?* She closed her eyes, tight, in the illogical hope of creating invisibility.

She heard footsteps getting closer and stop. Dirt tumbled down from above her, over the lip of her shelter. The settling dust irritated her nose.

She knew he stood directly above her. She willed herself to stop breathing. If he walked down into the gully, he would see her. More footsteps, as someone joined the doctor.

"Ella no está aquí."

"¡Silencio!"

The wind rattled the dried vegetation. She closed her eyes and thought of Alex. *If I get out of here alive, I promise I'll...*

"¡Serpientes! ¡Muchas serpientes!" More, unintelligible words drifted into the increasing wind. The voices grew distant...disappearing. Snakes had saved her. She looked around to be sure none threatened her.

Rosaria knew the searing heat of the day would give way to the cold of the night. She pulled more dirt and stones over her body, rested her bra-cradled head, and felt surprisingly comfortable in her dry river bed.

Her mind drifted to Shady Oaks and the required weekly Conversation Circle. "Tell us what you did this week that was interesting," the facilitator always began. Alma's hand was, of course, the first one that shot up. "I helped in the kitchen making lunch sandwiches, and I cut off the crusts as a special treat."

"Good for you, Alma."

"I stabbed a Mexican doctor, ran away into the desert, and he's trying to find me and kill me."

"Good for you, Rosie."

With the darkness came a disquieting stillness. She burrowed deeper into the dirt, which still retained the warmth of the day.

"Rosariaaaaaa," echoed across the dusty terrain. Blinding sunlight trumpeted a new day. A woman's voice called out again. She peeked over the top of the ravine and saw María pivoting near the distant pile of signal rocks.

"Here!" Rosaria shouted. Pain shot through her middle.
María ran toward her. "Are you hurt?"

"I'm fine, just filthy."

"I have come with my nephew."

A dark truck sped toward them, a cloud of dust in its
wake. María's arm encircled Rosaria's waist, as she guided her
up the river bank.

The truck bounced and bucked over the uneven ground. Each
bump sent pain searing through Rosaria's body. Between
leaps, Rosaria gulped down water.

"Eat this slowly," María said, as she handed her a corn
tortilla. Rosaria sat in the middle, between María and the
young male driver. She studied his face. Had he reached legal
shaving age, let alone driving age? The boy hunched over the
wheel and leaned toward the cracked windshield with fierce
concentration, keeping his foot flat on the accelerator, taking
it off when the truck flew into the air, and gunning it again
when the truck wheels smashed into the ground.

María patted Rosaria's arm, murmuring, "Está bien."

Far up ahead, Rosaria saw a few vehicles and no dust—a
paved road.

"Where are you taking me?"

"To my family," María replied.

I am safe.

Chapter 7

What was that smell? Ah, bleach. She knew from experience that the memory of smells stayed with her for a long time. Even all these years later, passing a florist and smelling lilies evoked sad memories of Longino's funeral. Some days she couldn't bear it and crossed the street before she got to the florist's outdoor displays. Today, the smell of bleach brought her mother back to her. Mamá leaning into their wooden outhouse, splashing bleach onto every exposed surface until the interior glistened. She even tossed some up onto the ceiling. Mexican women swore by bleach. It killed germs and bugs. And it was cheap.

She pushed away the heavy blanket; saw a roll of clothing emerge from beneath; and recognized her laundered blouse, skirt, and undergarments. Within the clothing, she found her bottles of pills and the fat envelope of bills.

A small wooden crucifix hung on the wall above her small bed. Beneath it, taped in place, was a page torn from a magazine, a faded Virgin Mary weeping beneath her son's cross. *Good morning, Mary and Jesús. What've I got to complain about?*

She needed a bathroom.

María sat on the porch, husking corn. "Rosaria! You're up!" María took her arm and guided her down the steps and along a rock-paved path to the outhouse. "Lo siento. This is all we have."

"This is all I need," Rosaria replied.

María's cousins were introduced—Rosa María, Consuela María, Graciela María, Estrella María—eight names in all, but she gave up trying to remember them. Rosaria had only to call "María!" and one or more women would run to her. They treated her with the respect they had decided a heroine of her stature deserved. Whatever her María had told them, it had impressed them. If they'd had a picture of Rosaria, she was certain the Virgin Mary's would be torn down and Rosaria's would replace her over each cousin's bed. Heady stuff for an old lady. Rosaria had only to raise her head, and one of them was there, inquiring what la Señora Rosaria desired. She felt like she was staying at a five-star resort, rather than at a modest family village.

The almost exclusively female enclave confounded Rosaria at first. Rojo, the young truck driver, was the only male around, except for the boy babies and pre-teens. She knew María, like herself, was a widow. Where were the other men? Obviously, there had been some at one time, for Rosaria didn't think there had been any Immaculate Conceptions recently. The explanation emerged during long mornings working in the vegetable garden and longer afternoons preparing their harvest for meals. As the women worked, they talked. Rosaria realized the women forgot she was among them—that her American accent and hesitant, long unused Spanish led them to believe she didn't totally understand. But she did comprehend enough, and what she heard shocked and saddened her. They talked about their men. Who had called, who had sent money. Who had not called, who had not sent money. Apparently, there were more of the latter. There was no paying work for the men here. Out of necessity, the men had migrated north, slipping across the border into the United States. A few had done it legally, for they had relatives living in Southern California who welcomed them into their homes. But most put themselves in the hands of paid smugglers of humans, a dangerous alternative.

When the women did not hear from their men, they feared the worst. And sometimes their fears were validated. The women gathered on María's porch, and whispered news, bad news. Word got back to them that two men had acquired new wives, with new babies on the way. Rosa María and Graciela Maria clung to each other and sobbed. They seemed ashamed of their common plight, and embarrassed to share their anguish with the other women. The others hurried away from them to their household tasks, murmuring softly "lo síento." *I'm sorry.* Secretly thinking, *Thank God it's not me.*

As the weeks passed into months, Rosaria relaxed more. She ceased fearing the evil doctor after the women showed her their rifles. These Marías would protect her. Each day, she woke to more sunshine, a clear head, and a calm stomach. Sunshine, she had expected. Her physical well being she attributed to the good women of María's village. They had passed around her bottles of pills, struggled to pronounce the names printed on the labels, and shook their heads. "No wonder la Señora Rosaria's mind doesn't work," they agreed. *My mind doesn't work?* Each day they gave her fewer of the offending medications until she was weaned. In their place, they fed her concoctions from their gardens—brewed teas, and pungent vegetable stews. They extolled the value of garlic and cooked with it, heavily...until she smelled it seeping from her pores. Eventually, she was immune because they all emitted the same odor. She began to feel more energy. Long lost words, English and Spanish, revisited her tongue, and her stomach digested whatever she fed it.

Instead of lazing on the porch chair, she ventured into the yard. Chickens pecking in the dirt cocked their heads when she clucked to them. She strolled to the end of the pathway and back. Bending down gingerly, she picked up a fist-sized rock and raised it over her head, mimicking the morning exercise routine at Shady Oaks. "Lift, ladies, lift! Men, get it up!" Rosaria remembered the two exercise leaders exchanging smirks, as if no one else got their innuendo. Rosaria grabbed another rock in her left hand.

"Lift, ladies, lift!" Up went her left arm. "Men, get it up!" Her right arm punched the air. She paced back and forth, shouting out her mantras. The chickens squawked and scattered.

"Rosaria, what are you saying?" María called from the porch.

Rosaria stopped with one arm raised and turned toward her. "Nothing."

To repay the kindnesses of the women, she helped them water and weed the plants in their vegetable gardens—sweet potatoes, squash, tomatoes, and corn. She shared her mother's recipes with them, too, and helped them make them. She held and comforted their fretful babies. In this place, she was a revered and valued woman; and she felt like her old self again, strong in body and mind, the woman she had been before her illness forced her to depend on others.

Anger at Alex still simmered to the surface, but she tempered it with compassion. She had a part in what had happened. Because she had stubbornly hidden her ability to speak again and her improved mobility, he had given up on her recovery. He didn't know. *I should have left him a note. But I was so angry—at him for what he had done—and at myself for what I hadn't done.* She would write a long letter to her son. Later. From Flores Bonitas.

After another month, Rosaria knew she was healed when she could laugh at the children's antics without clutching her rib cage. Her determination to get moving grew. She felt like a seasonal bird sensing the call to fly homeward. Although she would miss these beloved women, she needed to leave. And dear Alex? Home, to her, was south, not north. *I'll carry him with me, in my heart, to Flores Bonitas, my birthplace. I'm doing what I know is best for me, for both of us.*

Would Flores Bonitas be like she remembered, olive trees and yew-leaf willows filled with brilliant vermillion fly-catchers and white-winged doves? Whirling hummingbirds dipping to kiss flaming bougainvillea? The sea alive with stately seabirds: cormorants, reddish egrets, brant geese, and long-billed curlews? It had been so many years. In the many years since her mother's funeral, she hadn't been back. But would she at least recognize her village? Had her parents' casa survived?

Would the smells of neighbors frying corn tortillas fill the afternoon air? She wanted to inhale the briny breezes sweeping off the Sea of Cortez again. She wanted to stand on the beach and look back from the sea to the jagged mountains in the distance. Her heart stirred.

María marshaled her best arguments. "Señora, por favor. You should not be alone."

"You forget. I am a strong woman, a fighter of men!" Rosaria made a slashing motion, followed by the sign of the cross. *God forgive me for boasting about hurting another.*

"Sí, Rosaria. It is true. You are a strong woman."

The last morning, Rosaria took María and Juan into her arms for a long hug. María would be fine, here among her relatives. Rosaria held out a tattered envelope to María. She opened the flap to show her a stack of bills.

"No, Rosaria, I cannot."

"Take it for Juan. Por favor."

Juan reached out; and Rosaria put the envelope in his hand. He grabbed it and pulled it toward his mouth.

"Gracias, mi amiga," María said.

"You and Juan will come see me soon in Flores Bonitas."

Rojo bounded up the porch steps, eager to begin the adventure of driving Rosaria home. His longest trip had been to rescue Rosaria from the desert. Using money Rosaria gave him, he had filled the tank with fuel, and tied another can of gas to the bed of the truck. Two large containers of water and a bag of food rounded out their supplies. Their journey wasn't far, half a day, but in Mexico you never knew. Rojo took Rosaria's arm and led her to the truck.

Rojo eased the truck out of the yard, careful not to stir up dust and incur the wrath of the women. Just beyond the yard, he floored it and leaned on the horn. "Hasta la vista!" he called to the women waving from the porch.

Rosaria extended her feet, but could not reach the floorboard. She braced herself with one hand against the door and the other on the seat. She recalled the childhood lessons she learned riding a bucking burro, and relaxed her body into the truck's dips and jumps. She would not tell Rojo to slow down. Each turn of the tires took her closer to home.

Chapter 8

Alex gave a quick nod to the uniformed officer behind the counter, who nodded back. Alex continued down the familiar station hallway to Detective Sampson's desk.

The detective ran his hands through his long black hair. "What's up?" he asked.

"That's what I'm here to ask you," Alex replied.

"Nothing to report. I told you I'd call. You didn't need to drive all the way down here."

Alex held out a photo. "Here's a better picture I found of Mom, more of a close-up." His mother's face took up the entire four by six snapshot, her floppy hat brim blown up at the front, and her face a map of smile-line creases.

"Thanks, Alex, I'll add it to my collection." He gestured to a pile of photos piled under his computer monitor.

"I'd like you to display it," Alex said. He propped the photo against the bottom of the detective's monitor. "That way you won't forget her."

"You've been in here every week."

"Every other week. I write the date down every time. Today's week 31, day 217." He gave him a long look. "That way, I don't forget."

"It takes time." Detective Sampson slapped a haphazard stack of files.

"She's an old lady who needs to be found."

"You must know, Alex. Stats on finding her aren't good."

Alex knew the grim statistics by heart, thanks to multiple computer searches. The odds of finding a missing person dropped by 50% after 48 hours. After that, the odds dropped by 2% an hour, until...

"My mom's not a statistic. Keep searching for her. I'll be back."

"Sure, Alex." Detective Sampson turned back at his computer screen.

His mother would be the exception. She would be found...alive.

Alex pulled into his driveway, slammed his truck into park, and turned off the ignition. Resting his head against the steering wheel, he willed himself to breathe slowly and regularly. No point taking his anger out on Judith. It wasn't her fault, although he wanted to blame her. She had found the brochure for Shady Oaks. She had called to find out if they had an opening. She had pushed him to go see the place with her. She had brought it up again and again—how they had to reserve the room for Rosaria right away before it was taken—how he should sell his mother's house to pay for it.

But he had agreed. He signed all the papers. He told himself there was no alternative. After her stroke, his active and witty mom vanished, replaced by a stooped and shrunken old woman who shuffled and could no longer speak. She had lost weight, and her face had narrowed, her nose sharpened. Her eyes looked lifeless, like she had given up and already left him. How much of her brain was left functioning? The doctors showed him MRI's and pointed, but told him nothing definitive. *Time would tell*, they said.

In the meantime, days, weeks, months had gone by, and his mom was out there somewhere. *How long could she survive on the streets alone?* Autumn was giving way to winter, and its cold nights. When he couldn't sleep, he stared out into his slumbering neighborhood, putting a hand on the window pane to gauge the outside temperature. Sleep would be elusive for him again tonight.

From his vehicle, he saw Judith's face appear at the living room window.

"You all right?" she asked when he entered the house.

"That damn detective is sitting on his butt and doing nothing to find Mom."

Alex turned into the familiar street, stopped halfway down the block, and cut the motor. After his mother's disappearance, he had sought comfort obsessively in the old neighborhood; and he was back again today, to this place where he and his mom had been happy together. For these long months, on days when he should have been on a job site, he sat, instead, in his truck parked on his old street. From his customary vantage point, he had felt summer fade into autumn and winter, the days shortening. He had watched Tom Matthews paint beige paint over the blue exterior, and mourned every brush stroke that covered up the history of his childhood home. What had been a spindly pepper tree when he was a kid had grown thicker, and the eucalyptus tree out back towered over the house. Alex rolled down his window and inhaled the scent of the neighborhood. Even the air pollution smelled like home to him.

Chapter 9

Rojo tipped his head toward her and smiled. "Estamos aquí," he said.

We are here.

He pointed out the bug-speckled windshield to a dusty town square, motionless in the afternoon sun. A few mud-colored dogs stretched flat in the shade of a stone wall. Adobe and wooden store fronts ringed a small plaza, with a stone statue of a robed figure in its center. As they got closer, Rosaria recognized the Virgin Mary, a trickle of water dripping from her right eye and down her cheek.

Rojo drove the truck in a circle around the plaza. He laughed and pointed to a trough of water behind Mary, and to the plastic tube snaking up her back.

A miracle's where you create it.

They passed two men on a wooden porch, their heads tilted back, mouths slack as they slept. They resembled an ancient painting titled *Old Men Sleeping*. Ah, siesta time.

"¿Donde?" asked Rojo.

"El hotel," answered Rosaria.

Tall, spiny cactus brushed the truck's sides, and Rosaria leaned away from the open window. They rounded a corner, and the pale turquoise Sea of Cortez filled the horizon. Rosaria's hands flew to her chest.

"I'd forgotten how beautiful it is," she said.

The road became sand and ran parallel to the sea. Rosaria inhaled deeply. Rojo braked in front of a pink adobe building. "El Hotel Bougainvillea" a board nailed above the doorway proclaimed in faded black paint. Thick vines with clumps of orange blossoms clung to the walls and framed the door.

In the small lobby, an old lady snoring softly slumped over a wooden desk. Rosaria touched her shoulder, and the woman sat upright.

After Rosaria paid for two rooms for a week, she handed a key to Rojo. Let him have some adventures: a meal out, some music, new friends, some fun. Living among all those women, so many eyes watching him, so many tasks expected of him, he'd grown straight from child to man. A little tequila and youthful companionship was what he needed, and deserved. She saw she was right when Rojo protested, politely and briefly, to leaving her behind. "I'll come next door to the cantina later for dinner," she told him. "I need a rest."

Rosaria sank into the stiff sheets for her siesta. She woke to sweat dripping down her face. Several quick splashes of water in the right spots, a change of clothes, and she cooled.

Voices floated out when Rosaria opened La Cantina's door. Rojo sat at the bar, a booted foot on the railing and one elbow on the bar top. When he saw her, he tipped back his hat and lifted his beer bottle. As he started to rise. Rosaria held up her hand to stop him. She moved across the room and sat down at a far table against the wall. Last thing he needed, to waste his evening on an old lady. As though Rosaria had conjured her, a whirl of color emerged from an interior door next to the bar. A young woman held aloft a large tray filled with platters of food, her thin arms raised in sinewy strength. Graceful as a ballerina, she swooped to the bar and slid each dish in front of a patron. Several men gave her appreciative stares which she ignored. Rojo pivoted his head to follow her movements, and then returned to his food.

Rosaria ordered spicy local foods that she hadn't eaten in years. "So what if it kills me," she told the youthful waitress.

"Oh, no, señora, I hope not," she replied, bowing low.

With her dinner, Rosaria drank a margarita, served in a glass the size of a goldfish bowl. A trio of Maríachi guitarists arrived, spotted her, the new face, and drifted her way. They surrounded her table and launched into a plaintive love song. The men sang in Spanish: "My love, stay with me this night. Clock! Clock! Stop! Stop!"

Clocks didn't stop, but she did have tonight to enjoy. Emboldened by the alcohol, Rosaria beat a rhythm with her spoon, and her voice sang out, "Clock! Clock! Stop! Stop!"

She swayed her head from side to side. This is living. Rojo tapped his beer bottle on the bar to the beat, all the while keeping his eyes on the young waitress as she made her rounds of the patrons.

The bar room spun as Rosaria tried to stay on her feet. She leaned against her dance partner, her hand around his waist, and clutched the fabric of his shirt. He was sweating, and his shirt was wet. Like a flouncing rag doll, she felt her feet leave the floor as her partner scooped her aloft and whipped her around. Rojo and the pretty waitress danced by her.

Later, how much later her mind refused to compute, someone's arms propelled her. She willed her feet to walk, to lift higher up the hotel's steps. At her room door, she turned. Her dance partner had been tall because her head had rested low on his chest, and she hoped he was handsome. She focused her eyes upward, and into the serious eyes of Rojo.

"Señora," he said. He shook his head, as though he were the adult here, and she the adolescent.

She wanted to match his seriousness with hers and tried to form a response. Instead, she met his eyes, threw back her head, and laughed.

She dug out her notebook and began to write: *Last night I danced the night away with a tall, handsome stranger.* She read what she wrote. Her conscious nagged her. After all, Mary was weeping just down the road. She had resolved to keep her journal honest. She wrote a big question mark over the word "handsome." Rosaria would find out the truth of that adjective another day, or night. Today stood before her, and she resolved to experience another new adventure, and to write her day's triumph on her growing list.

She walked past sad Mary, to a cobblestone walkway leading to the Church of Our Lady of Flores Bonitas, with its wooden cross pointing into the cloudless sky. Her parents' resting place was easy to find, marked by a spindly olive tree casting mottled shade over the graves. She bent to pull out a vine growing over her mother's gravestone but stopped. Her mother had cherished her garden. Let that greenery grow.

Names and dates, all that were left of two lifetimes lived simply and honorably. Who else was left to remember them? No one in California, for her parents had left there as soon as they retired, to return here, their birthplace. And no one here either. From where she stood, she read familiar names carved into stones. *A generation gone.*

Two small angels leaned against her parents' stones. Angel and Angelica, her sister and brother, both born and dead the same day. Rosaria had been born a year later, her parents' miracle baby, they called her. As a kid, she had envied her friends who had siblings, but, at the same time, selfishly enjoyed being an only child. She didn't have to share Mamá and Papá's love. However, at this moment, she grieved for the twins, who could have shared her memories and the remainder of her life. She was alone.

As she retraced her steps and returned to the seaside colonnade, people of all ages spoke a greeting to her, or at least nodded her way, and most returned her smile. *God bless my people. They honor their elders.* Old women, perhaps her age, but weathered and worn, bent over their embroidery work, sold from small sheds covered in palm fronds along the ocean walkway. Rosaria searched their lined faces for a recognition of long-ago playmates. She saw no one she knew, and no one seemed to know her. *I'm being silly. We've all changed too much over the years.*

Rosaria browsed the displays and bought brilliant, primary colored serapes to fling over her shoulders in the evening chill, flowing cotton skirts, and peasant blouses blossoming with bright stitched flowers. Whatever the women asked for, she paid. One exuberant seller clasped Rosaria's money to her bosom and then waved it aloft in celebration. Another pitied her ignorance, and tried to teach Rosaria the art of negotiation. "I say 'ocho, es eight," she said, "and then you say...," gesturing for Rosaria to respond with a lower figure. But Rosaria didn't care; she knew she was paying way over the going rate. Some vendors gifted her with extra items—scarves, coin purses, floral hair pieces.

Hello world! Great shopping! No slips! No bras! She wrote on her list of adventures that night.

Tall, dark, and maybe handsome didn't present himself that night at the cantina, although the waitress who introduced herself as Adriana assured her that he was, indeed, very handsome, and very important. Oh, well, perhaps mañana. *I'm not going anywhere.*

Mañana. She ventured from the promenade to walk on the beach and removed her shoes. The warmth and softness of the sand was just as she remembered. The sea streamed onto the shore, leaving it cleansed and smooth. Other than so many sun umbrellas, her childhood beach appeared the same. She felt like the young girl she had once been, ready to plunge into the frothy surf. "Hey, come back when you grow up!" fresh boys had yelled her way. Then she had been embarrassed by her skinny, little-girl legs. Now she pulled up her skirt, exposing her shriveled, old-lady legs. "All grown up now, boys!" she called into the wind.

A few feet away, a toddler boy threw himself onto his back, flapped his arms and legs, and created a miniature sand angel. He stood up to admire it, kicked at the sand, and it was obliterated. When she was sure he was watching her, Rosaria stretched out on her back, swung her arms and legs in slow wide arches, and created her own angel. The boy covered his face and ran to the woman with him, pointing to Rosaria.

Rosaria walked inland from the ocean, along a pebble-strewn path. After 15 minutes or so, she stopped. There it was. Her parents' stucco home still stood, although a battered version of its former self. *Sort of like me, still standing.* The clematis, wild with purple blooms, remained along the shady side, right where Mamá had planted it. Its vines reached through the broken shutters, into the interior, as if to see who was home. No one was, and no one had been for a long time. Rosaria stepped up the rock stairs leading to the front porch. The wooden front door hung at a crooked angle. When she pushed it, the door toppled inward and crashed to the floor, sending dust flying. Rosaria stepped back and covered her face. When the dust had settled, she peered into her parents' house. Tattered remnants of floral curtains fluttered in the windows. Graffiti slashed across the interior walls, and broken bottles and crushed cans littered the floors. Gaping holes in the floor opened to the sandy soil beneath. She eased herself down to the porch ledge, draped her legs over, and swung her legs back and forth.

Chapter 10

Rosaria realized she had to get her money into a bank, before it was too late. She feared that Mexican banks might not be very secretive or stable; she didn't trust them completely. Did they even have insurance? She wasn't sure. Despite her misgivings, when she handed over the cashier's check to the bank teller, several days after her arrival in Flores Bonitas, she exhaled. She felt lighter.

When the young teller saw the amount, he called over the bank's manager, Señor Quiros, an older gentleman so genteel Rosaria expected him to take her hand in his and kiss it. He didn't. Both men escorted her into a private room with a long rectangular table that almost filled the interior. *The sum of my life. I did good.*

With the exchange rate down here, Rosaria was a rich woman. She could live comfortably, for a long time; and she intended to do both. She opened a checking account of 199,000 pesos, a savings account of 331,000 pesos, and converted a few hundred dollars to pesos for carrying around money. Despite the protestations of the manager, she sat with him as he electronically transferred the balance of her money to First California Bank in San

Gabriel, California, invested in a one-year certificate of deposit.

The manager perked up when she asked for a recommendation of a real estate agent. He walked her to the front door and pointed to a building across the street. *Quiros y Quiros* was painted in broad strokes on the window. As she turned to ask him if he was related, she saw he was already on his cell phone, his back to her. Although his voice was low, she heard him announce her imminent arrival to the realtor (a brother? a cousin?) across the way. She caught the words spoken in Spanish, "an old American woman with much money."

Why did so many people equate old with stupid? She drew herself up to her full five feet three inches and strode with purpose, in the opposite direction.

Señor Quiros, bank manager, called after her. "¡Señora! ¡Señora! ¡Por favor!"

She kept walking. Let him think she was old, stupid, and deaf. Adriana would steer her to another realtor, preferably a woman.

I like the way my homeland does business. They know how to get things done. With a flash of paperwork, prepared by the efficient Señora Espinosa, and a check for 87,534 pesos, Rosaria became the owner of her childhood home. Dual Mexican and US citizenship permitted her to own the property outright, in her own name. Foreigners had to buy using a fidelcomiso, a real estate trust held by a Mexican bank.

She was not a foreigner. Alex, too, as her son, qualified for dual citizenship. Did he know? She suspected he wouldn't be pleased. As a little boy, he had wanted all things American, nothing Mexican. He had refused her homemade tortillas. "Mom, make me a hot dog," he had said, "in a hot dog bun you buy at the store."

No handyman ads were necessary. Men waited for her each morning seeking work, some arriving before the sun was up. They squatted in small groups in the dappled early morning light outside the hotel. When she appeared, they scrambled to their feet and crowded around her, shouting. She pointed to half a dozen men who held up tools, and waved the rest away. As she walked along the long path to her home, the chosen ones followed, close on her heels.

Others ran up and darted across her path. "¡Señora! ¡Señora!" She couldn't hire them all so she ignored them and walked with purpose. At the edge of her property, she shouted "¡Por favor, vayan a todos ustedes!" to the rejected men. They retreated as far as the tall brush just beyond her yard, squatted down, and watched.

She led her hired men to the doorstep of her dilapidated home and issued orders. *Start with the floor, then the walls and ceiling. Finally, the roof and exterior.* As they worked, a few turned out to be real artisans, carving intricate designs into her new interior pillars. Rosaria allowed them their craftsmanship and their own time frame. She knew the pay they earned went a long way to supporting their large extended families. When one workman disappeared, she suspected she had paid him enough to live in grandeur... for a time...maybe for the rest of his life. She laughed at the thought and chose another man from the men who waited just outside her yard.

At times her comprehension could not keep up with the rapid Spanish fired at her by the men, and she asked them to speak slower. More of her Spanish was coming back to her, but she sometimes hesitated, searching for the right words. She had learned Spanish first as a child, then English, and now she feared her Spanish sounded stilted and accented. Some workers thought she didn't understand any of their conversations, or forgot she was around, or didn't care.

As she came up the steps, she heard Spanish that she translated internally. *This old woman has much money. Who wants to be her man?*

The men around him hooted, but quieted when they saw her.

"Young man, you need to apologize to me."

He smirked.

"Get out. Now. And never come back."

He grabbed up his tools and pushed past her. "Adiós, bruja vieja," he said.

Old witch. Her chest tightened. Rosaria looked straight ahead as she walked through the hushed workmen. She closed her bedroom door behind her, leaned against it, and put her hands to her chest. Beneath her blouse, her heart thumped.

She willed herself to breathe in-out, in-out, until her heart settled into a gentle rhythm. No sound of workers. Had they all left? She opened her door. The workmen, freeze-framed in place, sprang to life. Hammers whacked at nails, and saws whined through wood.

"¡Buen trabajo!" Rosaria said. *Good work!*

As soon as the broad new floorboards were in place, Rosaria moved out of the hotel room and into her childhood bedroom. Although her parents' bedroom was larger, she couldn't bring herself to occupy it, not yet anyway. Mamá and Papá were still present in this house—their room a holy place. Mamá often stopped by. Papá came less frequently, watchful and quiet. Mamá had lots to say:

Rosaria, you always were such a good girl.

Rosaria, my heart fills to see you here.

Rosaria, plant more flowers and some vegetables.

Rosaria, time to sit on the porch and rest.

Two men delivered and deposited her new bed flat against an inner wall, but Rosaria pointed to the center of the room, and told them to re-position her bed there, its foot almost touching the windowsill. The headboard jutted out into the center of the room, an unconventional arrangement. However, from her bed, she could see the view outside her window, framed by the newly trimmed ancient clematis. Dirt dominated out there, but she would plant a garden, as Mamá suggested. Rosaria had planted seeds in small clay pots that lined the front of her porch, and hopeful green plants pushed out the soil in each. She hadn't needed to label them. As they grew, she recognized their leaves: bean, pea, tomato, and zucchini.

A lamp atop a small table next to her bed lit the books she read each night—tattered, second-hand romance novels written in Spanish—bought from a woman who sold used household items and paperbacks.

"Este es un buen libro," the woman would say, drawing out 'buen' as she held out the *good book*, its cover art depicting the requisite bosomy woman swooning in a bare-chested man's arms.

"¿Te gusta?" Rosaria asked.

"Mis ojos son malos," she replied, raising her sunglasses to reveal her eyes, both clouded with the milky film of cataracts.

"Lo siento, señora. Mi nombre es Rosaria. ¿Y su nombre?"

"Ynez."

Each time she returned, Ynez pumped Rosaria with questions. *Did she like the book? What happened? Did they turn out to love each other? Did the señorita and the señor... you know?* She giggled and hid her mouth behind her hand.

Rosaria's recent reading research had shown that the more exposed the bosoms on the cover, the more graphic the novel's lovemaking. No wonder Ynez favored those books. As Rosaria read in bed at night, she began to fold down pages to read to Ynez the next day.

After Rosaria got her workmen started each day, she hurried along the path to Ynez and read to her. Ynez pulled out a second plastic chair from beneath her cart and told Rosaria to take a seat. The few turned-down pages no longer satisfied Ynez. At the slightest pause, she said, "Más, por favor," and she gestured for Rosaria to keep reading. As Rosaria read, Ynez scraped her own chair closer, until her knees almost touched Rosaria's. She sat so motionless that Rosaria glanced up at Ynez's bamboo thin chest to be certain she was still breathing. When the occasional customer stopped, Rosaria learned to stop reading so Ynez would conduct business. If she didn't stop, Ynez ignored them; and Rosaria was certain she couldn't afford that. The pre-owned kitchen utensils, plastic bowls, and paperbacks, weren't going to sell themselves. For the most part, Ynez haggled with vigor when she bought and sold. The very young and the very old got much better deals.

Like an old-time vaudeville audience, Ynez booed the evil villains, cheered the brave heroes, and wept for the endangered heroines. People who stopped to browse at Ynez's cart began to linger and joined in Ynez's responses. Before long, other sellers left their carts to see what the fuss was about. Rosaria's audience grew each day, and she had to raise her voice to reach the people in the back. One day, after many pages, Rosaria faltered, her mouth dried out, and her back sore.

"Aquí, Rosaria," Ynez said. She thrust a fist-sized fruit into Rosaria's hand, and leaned forward and pulled a pillow from behind her back.

"Qué es?" Rosaria asked as she held up the fruit.

"Mamey."

Rosaria peeled back the brown skin and licked the fleshy orange pulp. "¡Mamey es delicioso!" Rosaria said as she bit into the sweet fruit.

Ynez motioned for Rosaria to lean forward, and eased the pillow behind her. "Sentirse bien?"

Rosaria sank back against the pillow. "Sí, muy bien."

Ynez pointed to the book. "Más, por favor," she said.

"¡Sí!" others echoed.

Rosaria took a deep breath and read on.

Ynez's way of thanking Rosaria—and planning their next book—was to slip an extra book, one with ample bosom and manly chest, into her bag of daily purchases. Rosaria was careful to carry one of Ynez's choices along when they were about to finish one book and begin another. When they finished a book, Rosaria handed it back to Ynez to resell. Often someone in the crowd would buy it, on the spot. Sometimes bidding wars erupted.

As the renovations occurred around her, Rosaria didn't mind some dust. Her favorite time of day was when the last workman had gone; and she moved from room to room, caressing the gleaming new wood and inhaling its scent. After the exertion of reading aloud at Ynez's cart, Rosaria sank into her bed each night, exhausted, beneath a woven blanket in muted pastels, bought from Ynez. The long fringes of the blanket tickled her nose. She fought to stay awake and read, but sleep won.

No closets in her little home. That wasn't the Mexican way. Instead, wooden pegs on the walls held a family's clothing. Her rooms were small and would become smaller if Rosaria had her men build closets for her. In her small bedroom, she had a workman build and place against a wall a wooden wardrobe for her clothing, hand carved vines twisting down its sides. She hung her bright new garments on a short rod. Shelves built within the cabinet held the remainder of her clothing: cotton underpants for decency and woven serapes for warmth and a touch of glamour. Rosaria loved to sweep open the double doors and admire the colorful contents.

She sure didn't miss bras and slips, but she pined for the floral bathing suit she'd left behind when they fled the doctor. Ynez and the other vendors did not sell such an exotic item. After Rosaria shared her dismay with Adriana, she took Rosaria's hand and led her to a back room in the cantina. A computer screen glowed on a desk. Adriana's hands flew over the keyboard, and a replacement suit was ordered.

Every day Rosaria walked to the cantina anticipating its arrival. She awaited the day she could flip her dress up over her head, astound the beach crowd with her suit, and plunge into the surf. Maybe she was well past plunging, but she'd sure walk in up to her waist. *La Señora Loca Del Mar, that's me.* She liked the sound of it: *The Crazy Lady of the Sea.*

The next day, Rosaria handed one of her more skilled workmen a wooden board and a piece of paper.

"What do you wish, señora?" he asked.

"Carve these words, please," she replied. She pointed to

the spot above the exterior door where she wanted him to hang the completed sign.

"Are you certain this is what you wish, señora?"

"Yes, and put some roses around the edges, too, please," Rosaria said.

He tipped his head in her direction. "I will be pleased to do so, señora."

Ever since she had fired the rude young man, the conversations she overheard from the remaining workmen were about the work in progress. When they approached her for instructions, they spoke in distinct, careful Spanish.

She made certain to express her appreciation for their good work. "¡Gracias! ¡Buen trabajo!" she said to each worker as he left for the day.

As she read to Ynez and the others each day, she made sure she announced her pleasure at the work being done on her home. News spread fast in a small village, and she wanted to frame the message. She knew that the men she didn't hire, and those she fired, resented her. Some of them lurked among the men waiting outside her yard. Seeing them there made her uneasy.

Chapter 11

One night she dreamed again. Alex appeared as a toddler, lost on a strange street.

"Mom! Mom!" his high-pitched voice cried as he ran a zigzag path away from her.

She struggled to run toward him, but her legs felt like weighted sacks of rice. He continued to run and sob, his voice fading to a sad broken record, as she stood pinned in place and watched him disappear. She woke crying during the night. The full moon lit her front yard and cast shadows, and she peered within them for lurking men, but saw no one.

In the morning, the dark sorrow of her dream stayed with her. She had been too occupied to think much about Alex. And when she had thought of him, anger, justified anger in her mind, surged through her. How dare he lock her away when she was too weak and sick to resist? He took the easy way out—didn't stand up to Judith. Rosaria had stepped back when he married, tried to embrace Judith's presence in their lives. But Judith, ever prickly, never softened to her.

But her dream turned her thinking about Alex on its

head. *I refused to speak to him, because I wanted to punish him, to inflict guilt on him for putting me away in that place. I didn't even leave him a note. My poor boy. Is he searching for me? How can I let him know I'm safe and all right?*

Wait a minute.

And what if Alex did find her, and took her back to that half life? She shivered in the warm air. She remembered him, rushing in from work to squeeze in yet another obligatory visit. She imagined him, his eyes full of sadness and pity. *Forgive me, dear son. I don't think you and I can bear more of that.*

Rosaria decided to shake off her dour mood by walking into town and treating herself to a plate of rice and beans at the cantina. That's what she needed: fresh air, exercise, nourishment, a talk with Adriana. And maybe her bathing suit had arrived? That would cheer her up.

On the path into town, she heard shouts ahead and hurried toward them. About a dozen men, crouched in a circle, slapped their straw hats into the dusty ground. In the center of their circle, she could make out flapping wings. The wings separated into two roosters, stalking each other for their next strike. Back at each other they flew, and Rosaria caught a glimpse of shiny metal. Razors for spurs...*I remember.* When blood spurted into the dirt, heat flushed up her neck into her face, and her stomach lurched.

"Only small men prove their manhood using defenseless birds," Rosaria said in English.

"Go away, old woman," one said. The man speaking stood up and advanced toward her.

She turned and walked away with measured steps. A bottle crashed into the brush near her. Her hands trembled. She hugged them to her body and kept walking. Around a bend in the path, she picked up her pace. She arrived at the cantina with sweat dripping down her face.

"Estás bien?" Adriana asked from behind the bar.

"I just walked too fast in this heat," Rosaria said, speaking slowly and enunciating clearly.

Adriana guided Rosaria to a chair and brought her a tall glass of water. "¿Almuerzo?"

"Not hungry," she said. "Did my bathing suit arrive?"

"Rosaria. I need to say...cómo se dice...algo muy importante?"

"You, no, *I* need to say something very important."

"Pero..." Adriana said.

Rosaria gave Adriana a hard look.

Adriana blew out air. "I need to say something very important."

"Good English!"

Adriana held up her hand. "Stop, por favor."

Rosaria wanted to correct her scrambled language, but Adriana's urgent tone stopped her. She sat down.

"Men come to bar and talk. They say, la señora es loca."

"I'm not afraid of some men talking in a bar," Rosaria said. She straightened her back and sat taller.

Adriana grabbed both Rosaria's hands. "Say la señora has mucho dinero...."

"Maybe someone at the bank told them."

"Señora, the men say su dinero está en su casa."

"That's not true. I don't keep money at home," Rosaria said.

"Rosaria, men say yes. And you are alone."

Rosaria attempted a laugh and pulled her hands out of Adriana's. "I can take care of myself. I have done a good job so far."

"Señora, you must hear. You are not…invincible."

On the walk back home, her appetite returned, and she looked forward to heating up the take-out meal Adriana had thrust into her hands as she left. As she approached her porch, buzzing flies alerted her. She saw a carcass on her top step. Had one of the roaming cats left her a gift? When she got closer, she recognized the bloodied feathers of a rooster. Her vision blurred, and she gripped the railing to keep her balance. She drew in a deep breath, stepped around the dead creature, and held her breath until she got to the far edge of her porch. Adriana's meal slipped from her hands; the pottery dish broke, beans and rice spilled onto the floor. Rosaria leaned over the edge of her porch railing and vomited.

The joke was on her, reveling in her craziness, only to find the local people were literal. To them, the carved plaque over her door labeled her who she was, *The Crazy Lady of the Sea*, and a foolish old one, at that. And she had been careless, throwing around her money, without thinking about her vulnerability. Despite her childhood ties to this place, she was a foreigner to them, an American.

That night Rosaria went to sleep in her little house afraid.

The next morning, Rosaria sat on her front porch drinking coffee and eating small bites of a corn tortilla. As the workmen filed into her yard, a dog's huge muzzle peeked out from the growth outside her gate, directly opposite where the unemployed men sat. She recognized the shy stray from her walks into the village and to the beach. One of the men threw a rock at him, and he disappeared.

Rosaria opened the gate, walked to the edge of the brush, and threw a piece of her tortilla into the growth. She heard chewing. After she dropped another piece of her tortilla on the open ground, a lowered head appeared. "Ven aquí, perro," she said in a soft voice. She dropped more tortilla bits behind her. When she got inside the gate, she threw the remainder of the tortilla near the porch. The dog ran past her, and she closed the gate.

Rosaria kept the name the local people had given him: Diablo. *Devil.*

Food and soft words convinced him she would not harm him. Within a few days, he trusted her enough to sprawl out close to her, and allowed her to stroke his head. Her workmen stepped wide round him, and the men outside her fence eyed him warily. When Diablo stood next to her, his head came to her elbow. Rosaria tried to identify the breeds that made up this magnificent animal. If she had to label him, he was Doberman-Shepherd-Wolfhound. His ears stood high and alert atop a head the size of a soccer ball, and his long muscular legs supported a thick body covered in long mottled gray and white hair.

Instead of Diablo, a more suitable name for the dog would have been Angel, for he was at heart a gentle creature, a secret Rosaria told no one. Whenever a workman approached her, she gripped Diablo's heavy leather collar with one hand and put her other hand over his big snout, as though he might at any moment leap for the throat of the man. She explained to the men that Diablo had been abused by men, undoubtedly the truth, and that he didn't trust them. The men backed away, keeping their eyes on the dog.

"Diablo bueno," Rosaria said. "Good Devil." He would be bi-lingual.

Nights she slept well. She no longer feared dangerous men. Hearing Diablo's soft snores from his mat near her bed, Rosaria's last conscious thoughts were of gratitude for her gentle companion.

Mornings she awoke to hot dog breath on her face and mournful brown eyes staring at her, the dog's muzzle resting on her pillow. Always the gentleman, he stood by her bed until she threw back her covers. Then he led the way to the kitchen, quick skittering steps on the polished wood floor, and waited for her to open the door. When he returned, he stood towering over his bowl, waiting for her to serve up his breakfast. After he slurped up the last morsel and licked his bowl, she wiped his hairy chin with a wet cloth. Afterward, Diablo lay down as if to say, *Now it's your turn to eat.*

So far as the dog was concerned, water was for drinking. Diablo took a long drink from the soapy wooden tub Rosaria had filled in the yard, and backed away in astonishment. He shook his sudsy wet snout and sneezed vigorously in her direction. She pulled him toward the tub, whispering to him. She brought the wet cloth onto his back, and massaged him gently and felt his tensed body relax. Filthy water dripped into the yard. She kept at it until the water off Diablo's back ran clear. Finally, Rosaria turned to a tub of plain water, and rinsed him. He shook vigorously and stood, as if to say, *Now what?* Rosaria rewarded him with a dog biscuit. Each week when she opened his tin of treats, he ran out to the tub, ready for his bath. "Perrro inteligente. Smart dog," Rosaria whispered in his big ears. His intelligence would be another of her secrets about him.

Rosaria settled back into the cushioned wood rocking chair. On the edges of the porch, her sprouting vegetable plants peeked over the tops of their containers, soon to be transplanted into her backyard garden. Workmen had laid a flat stone walkway from her porch to the gate. To line the new path, Rosaria had directed the planting of native plants, plucked from the jumble of growth along the path to the ocean. She liked the variety of cacti she chose, and that some of them—the organ pipe cactus and the barrel cactus—would grow from their present one-foot height to six feet or taller. These she had planted like a line of spinney sentries along the fence surrounding her property. Cat's claw vine, she planted at the base of each fence post. In the middle of her yard she planted tree ferns, agave, and many tiny unnamed plants that struck her fancy. Seasonal rain and occasional watering would be enough to nourish them.

Clicking nails announced Diablo's arrival on the porch. He trotted to her and dropped a yard-long length of heavy rope at Rosaria's feet, ready for their daily tug-of-war game. Rosaria picked up the rope and held on, tight. Diablo grabbed his end, and pulled, hard. He lowered his big head, dug in his front legs, and growled. Rosaria was pulled forward to the edge of her chair. "Perro bueno. Good dog."

After as many minutes of back and forth as her strength would allow, she let go of the rope. Diablo always won. He loved their game, and Rosaria loved that he associated the rope with tugging, and, more important—to her—with growling. Rosaria cut off a few inches of the rope, and kept it in her pocket. When she felt the least bit apprehensive—or just for the fun of it—she slipped the rope from her pocket. Without fail, Diablo ran to her, sniffed at the rope, and growled.

Petting Diablo comforted Rosaria. Each week she poured a little hair conditioner into his rinse water, and his thick coat softened and smelled better, unless he had found some irresistible dead creature to roll himself in. Even smart dogs liked to do dumb things. That just meant an extra bath…and an extra treat for Diablo. Aha. Outsmarted by the smarter creature.

Most days Rosaria continued her routine of walking to the ocean promenade and reading aloud at Ynez's stall. She attached a new leash to Diablo's collar, and took him along. Until she knew he could be trusted, she held his leash in a loose grip. Better to let him run off, rather than swept off her feet and injured. But Diablo ignored the allure of other dogs and distractions. He marched along, leaving the leash hang slack between them. He adored her, only her, and the feeling was mutual.

She discouraged her reading audience from petting Diablo. "Diablo le gustana los niños pero no los adultos y sobre todo no los hombres." As she spoke, she brought the bit of rope from her pocket and held it at Diablo's nose. "You like the children, but not the adults, and especially not the men, right Diablo?"

Good Dog Diablo growled right on cue. The grownups closest to her stepped back.

But despite her admonitions, she couldn't keep the little children away from him. As she began to read and directed her eyes to the book, the kids crept forward to the dog. A few gripped his neck in tight embraces, and some kissed his head. Diablo stood like a regal statue, enduring their affections. When he had enough, he licked their faces with his long, wet tongue, sending them squealing for their mothers.

As she always did the days she read, Rosaria fell into a deep sleep that night. Some hours later she awakened to low growling. "What is it, Diablo?"

Diablo bolted down the hall to the front door, with Rosaria shuffling as fast as she could in her flopping slippers behind him. He lunged up at the door again and again, and barked with an urgency that frightened her. She reached to grab his collar and pull him away, but he jerked his head up and out of her reach. Rosaria crept to her front window and eased a corner of the cotton curtain back a few inches. Bright moonlight illuminated two men running away along her front path. They flung her gate open and disappeared into the tangled growth. The gate swung back and forth, until it settled into a half-open position.

Rosaria stood and shivered while Diablo continued to bellow.

Chapter 13

The front door of his mother's former home opened, and another mother and son appeared in the doorway. Grace Matthews brushed back her son's bangs and kissed his forehead. Tommy bolted away across the lawn, his backpack flapping and ran past the truck. Alex turned away before the boy saw him. He didn't belong here. He felt like a stalker.

Why did he feel the need to return here, again and again? He knew he couldn't have his old life back. But he sure wanted his mom back. How could she just disappear? Not knowing if she was even alive tortured him. What did he seek from these people? *Their life. I want their life.* From where he was, peering in, they looked so happy—like the life he had lived here with his mother had been, like the life he wanted to re-create with Judith.

He left his truck and walked around the block toward the arroyo that backed up to the rear of the Matthews' yard. The wind swirled through the creek bed, where a slow trickle of water meandered between rocks. He scooped up a handful of pebbles, walked onto the footbridge, and whipped the stones into the water, trying to make them skip. How many hours had he spent back here with his buddies—tossing rocks, digging in the moist dirt, making forts? His mom had been fine with his adventures, except on those rare Southern California days when rain threatened. Then the gentle stream might turn into a tumbling wall of water. Mom wouldn't let him out of the house those days.

He threw his last stone and leaned against the wooden railing. His left hand felt a nail. A bit of fabric hung from it. He pulled it loose. As he stared at it absent mindedly, Snoopy's nose emerged, barely visible in the faded fabric. He spun around, peering in all directions. His hand shook as he pulled out his cell phone.

"I found…. I found…." He couldn't catch his breath.

"Alex, slow way down. What did you find?" Detective Sampson said.

"I found a piece of my mom's sweatshirt," he replied.

The next afternoon, Alex and the detective stood on the same walkway, leaning down toward the drainage canal.

"Dry now, but we had that big rain, day before your mother went missing. Couple inches in a couple hours. Water was rushing through here, up almost to this bridge," said Detective Sampson.

"Mom wouldn't be out here in the rain."

"There's more. We found pieces of women's clothing caught in those big rocks down there." He pointed to a jumble of boulders. "Your mother's name is on…like they do for laundry in those nursing home places."

"Did anyone actually see my mom?"

The detective grabbed Alex's arm. "Alex, the clothing was all torn up...like it had been tumbled over rocks."

"What're you telling me?"

"Sorry, but we think your mother...fell into the water and couldn't get out...got swept away. I'm sorry, Alex."

Chapter 14

Rosaria heated up a familiar and comforting breakfast, beans and rice. *Rosaria, this morning we're eating something different. Instead of rice and beans, we're having beans and rice!* Mamá's voice echoed in the tile-floored kitchen, so real that Rosaria looked over, expecting to see her mother's back bent over the wood-burning stove. Instead, a gleaming silver appliance sat in its place. And no Mamá, never to be replaced. Rosaria sniffed into her handkerchief.

Diablo snapped her out of her reveries. He had learned to pull his dangling leash down from the peg in the kitchen and bring it to her. If she didn't acknowledge him, he followed her, dragging the leash, until she took it from his mouth and snapped it on his collar. Each morning he stood vigil while she completed her simple morning routine. In the bathroom, she splashed water on her face, the full extent of her makeup. She slipped into the fresh underwear, clean blouse, and cotton skirt she had laid out the night before. Diablo was patient, so long as she moved. But when she sat on her bed to pull on her sandals, he stood over her—to be sure she didn't sink back into her bedding. She had tried that once, and Diablo had stepped a big paw on her chest and licked her face with his rough wet tongue, a canine version of Mamá's *rise and shine.*

How long had it been since she planned a party? Alex's birth-day parties, boisterous events of running, energetic boys stopped when he became a teenager. *Mom, no more crepe paper, balloons, and piñatas. Please,* he begged her. From then on, he and his buddies celebrated at a video arcade, with a cake devoured in the snack shop, after their coins were de-pleted. Rosaria had never, in her entire life, hosted a party for herself. *About time. I'll throw myself a blast of a homecoming party.* Rosaria retrieved her notebook from her bedside end table, and began to write her party shopping list: *Crepe paper! Balloons! Piñatas! Musicians!*

Rosaria grabbed her latest read-aloud material and headed out with Diablo on her heels. She wanted Ynez to be the first person she invited. As Rosaria turned to close the gate to her yard, she spied two beer bottles on the ground among her plants—evidence of last night's mauraders. Men made foolish by liquor. They would boast, if they remem-bered last night; and Adriana would tell her who they were. Until then, Rosaria had people waiting for her, her eager reading audience. She would worry about mañana when it arrived—mañana.

When Rosaria and Diablo emerged from the jungle path, the tarp-draped hulk of Ynez's cart stood against the ocean backdrop. Rosaria searched right and left along the promenade. Other men and women fussed at their carts, arranging their wares for the day ahead. Where was Ynez? She had no idea where Ynez lived. When she had asked her, Ynez replied with a flip of her hand gesturing to the north.

"Dónde vive Inez?" Rosaria asked a young woman with a pre-school boy who hid behind her skirt. She pointed to the north, keeping her eyes on the pavement.

When Rosaria had first arrived, she complained to Adriana about the rudeness of the villagers—never meeting her eyes in conversation. "They are showing respect to you," Adriana explained. "And some are simply shy."

"Por favor, lléveme a su casa," Rosaria said.

The young woman nodded and began to walk north along the promenade. Rosaria hoped she knew the way, that she wasn't merely displaying good manners to an older woman. Rosaria and Diablo fell into step behind her. "Cómo te llamas?" Rosaria asked.

"Carolina," she replied.

"¿Y su hijo?" Rosaria pointed at the little boy.

"Jesús."

"Jesús es un nombre muy importante," Rosaria said.

Jesús tilted his head up and smiled. He scrambled back around her to Diablo, and reached out to give him a quick pat along his rib cage. Diablo turned back to sniff him, and the boy ran to his mother.

Carolina led her off the promenade onto a narrow path. Rosaria walked with careful steps, watching for exposed tree roots. She had learned her lesson. A stroke had led to her incarceration. A fall could be fatal, or worse; and she'd end in one of those places again. Carolina turned at a still narrower path. Tangled growth tugged at their clothing as they made their way into a small clearing.

"Aquí es Inez," Carolina said.

"¿Aquí?" Rosaria said.

A shack, smaller than the tool shed the workmen had built for her, sat in the dirt. Rosaria's shed, built of sturdy wooden planks, offered more shelter than this.... Rosaria hesitated to call it a house. The walls appeared to be of cardboard, with ragged holes cut for windows. The roof was created with dried palm fronds, stacked in one direction, with another pile on top in the opposite direction, an attempt at rain-proofing. How did the cardboard support that weight?

Rosaria walked around. Where was the door? At the back, a faded floral fabric hung in a five-foot high opening. Rosaria wanted to knock, to announce her presence, but feared her fist on the fragile cardboard would bring it crashing down.

"¡Ynez! ¿Comó estas?" Rosaria called into the opening.

"Muy bien. ¿Y usted?" a soft voice said from within.

Rosaria pulled back the curtain, ducked, and entered. Ynez lay in a corner on a haphazard pile of blankets.

"¿Qué ha pasado?"

Ynez attempted to rise, but fell back.

Out the long habit of motherhood, Rosaria touched Ynez's forehead with her hand. It felt hot. As her eyes adjusted to the interior darkness, Rosaria saw sweat trickling down Ynez's face. She tried to remember the last time she had seen Ynez. Four days perhaps?

"Necesita un médico," Rosaria said.

"¡No! No necesito un médico."

Ynez pointed to the opposite corner, where a small charcoal burner sat, a kettle on its grill. "Té, por favor," she said.

"Phew. ¿Qué es esto, Ynez?"

"Té para curarme."

This tea cure you? More likely kill you. Rosaria watched Ynez struggle to raise her head and swallow the foul liquid. She fell back onto her bed, and closed her eyes.

Rosaria ran out into the yard. "Carolina, bring the doctor here. Ynez is very sick. Tell him I will pay. Hurry!"

"No comprendo."

"Lo siento," Rosaria said, and repeated her plea in Spanish.

"Sí, señora." Carolina swept Jesús up into her arms and ran down the path.

Rosaria pulled a low stool to Ynez's bed. Taking Ynez's hand in hers, she began to pray in a soft voice, healing petitions in the Spanish of her childhood.

Diablo barked.

A teenage boy pushed in through the curtained doorway. "What are you doing here?" Diablo's barking grew more frantic.

"I'm Rosaria, and—" she began.

"I know who you are." He straightened to his full height. "And who are you?"

"I am Ynez's grandson. I live here, and you need to leave."

"Your grandmother is very ill. I have sent for the doctor."

"Leave. Now." He grabbed her elbow and pulled her

to her feet. "I mean it." He squeezed her elbow, hard, and pushed her away.

Rosaria led Diablo a few feet away, still in sight of Ynez's home. They would wait here until the doctor arrived.

"Hey, I told you to get out of here." The young man advanced across the dirt.

Diablo growled and pulled on the leash.

"Stay back," Rosaria said.

"I'm not afraid of you, old woman, or that stupid dog of yours." He pointed a beer bottle at Diablo. "I know where you live."

The leash whipped out of her hand and flapped on the ground behind Diablo as he ran and then pounced. The boy fell to the ground, and the dog clamped his jaws onto the arm holding the bottle as he twisted his head. The bottle flew into the dirt.

"Stop him!"

"Diablo! Drop!"

Rosaria hurried over and picked up the leash. "Get up," she said.

"Your dog tried to kill me." He massaged his arm.

"If he'd wanted to, he would have."

Rosaria and Julio, as he had grudgingly identified himself, established a Mexican standoff of sorts. While Rosaria and Diablo kept vigil over Ynez, Julio watched them from the doorway.

From Ynez's shelf, Rosaria lifted a bowl to fill with water. As she did, a small photo slid from its standing position. Children stood on steps of a wooden building. She held the photo closer to see the children's faces, and saw her own. She stood, front and center, holding the hand of another smaller girl—her best friend Pajarito. *Birdie*, the nickname of this tiny, flitting person suited her. *I'm surprised she stood still long enough for the picture.* Both girls' dresses ended above their knees, and their socks sat in rumpled piles around their ankles. Rosaria turned over the photo. *Rosíta (Rosaria) y Pajarito (Ynez)* was printed in careful letters on the reverse.

Parajito! Could it be? During the past months, Rosaria had spent so many hours with Ynez—reading to her, talking with her—never realizing that this was *her* Ynez, *her* Parajito. Of course, they wouldn't recognize each other. Neither resembled the little girls they had been, but why had they never talked about their pasts? recognized their connection? They hadn't. To Ynez, Rosaria was a wealthy American woman, coming to Flores Bonitas to spend her final years. To Rosaria, Ynez was an aging local villager, supporting herself selling wares.

Why didn't Rosaria look for her as soon as she got to Flores Bonitas? She could have rescued her friend from her retched shack? *I was too caught up in myself and my problems. And all the time Parajito was suffering. She is sick because of my selfishness.* Rosaria clutched the photo tight against her chest and blinked away tears.

Her friend needed her. No crying. She dipped a rag into the bowl of water and placed it on her old friend's forehead.

"Pajarito, yo soy tu amiga Rosíta," she whispered. *I am your friend Rosíta.*

Pajarito's eyes fluttered and closed.

Chapter 15

The room was cold and quiet. Alex sat on the edge of the stiff leather chair. His legs bounced up and down until Judith put her hand on his knee, and he stopped.

"I'm so sorry for your loss," the young man said, his voice a whisper. He came around the desk and extended his hand. It was cold, too. His skinny neck stuck out of his too-wide collar, and his tie bunched up the fabric in a failed attempt to make it fit. He looked like a curious young turtle overextending its neck. *Why would any guy want to be an undertaker?*

Judith pressed into Alex's arm. "Alex?" she said.

Alex nodded and inhaled. This was going to be hard, too hard. He felt nauseous from the overpowering smell of flowers. "Men's room," he managed.

He splashed cold water on his face and bent over the sink. The nausea had passed, but his chest felt heavy with the weight of his grief. Now he knew what people meant when they said they were heartbroken. Surely his heart was torn in a jagged, bleeding line from top to bottom. He put his hand to his chest and was surprised to feel his heart beating. No one died of grief. He ripped a paper towel from the dispenser, pressed it to his face, and turned away.

"Alex, check out these flowers." Judith pointed to the first page of the brochure. "They get cheaper toward the back."

Vases held pastel flowers, with white lilies jutting out of the arrangements. That was what Alex smelled in this awful place—the lilies.

"Roses, red roses," Alex said. "Mom likes them."

The undertaker smiled benignly, as he had no doubt been trained. "Roses will be fine. Could I suggest an interspersing of baby's breath for contrast?"

Undertaker—what a strange word that was—literally taking someone under the ground. At least his mother would be spared that.

"Alex," Judith said. She held out a different pamphlet, this one showing gravestones.

Grave—another word that fit the occasion. Serious, solemn. He struggled to focus on the printed material, while his heart continued to pump and bleed.

People filed past him in the visitation room. He recognized some of them from St. Jude's. Many he knew since childhood and they greeted him as Alejandro. He replied to them in long unused Spanish. To honor his mother, he would be Alejandro today.

"Lo siento, Alejandro. Lo siento," they murmured.

He was sorry, too. Sorry for so much. He replayed the last time he had seen his mother. How small she seemed—shrunken after her stroke. Why hadn't he realized how unhappy she was? She must have been desperate to run out into the night to that bridge.

Father Rafael Jaramillo approached him. "Alejandro, we can begin."

Alex joined Judith in the first row. He stared straight ahead at the table covered with a white lace cloth. In its center, an 8 x 10 framed color photo of Rosaria stood in an upright frame, surrounded by two bouquets of crimson roses. In the picture, his mother wore her gardening clothes, a red and blue checked blouse and denim slacks. A short-brimmed straw hat topped her head. She held up a garden trowel in a mock threat to the photographer—her son. Her face crinkled in laughter, and the sun sparkled in her brown eyes.

She had scolded him for taking that picture of her, hair flying in the breeze and without lipstick. Perhaps she would have preferred a more dignified photo displayed today, maybe her studio portrait from the church directory. No, he wanted to remember her at her happiest, out in her yard. She loved her garden and joked she didn't have a green thumb—she had a brown one—from so much digging in the earth. Evenings before mass, she soaked her hands in a basin of hot water and cleaned the dirt from underneath her nails and buffed them to a shine.

Alex heard the rustling of people behind him. The undertaker and his helper scurried to bring in more folding chairs. People shifted on the carpeting to make room for additional seats. *Mom would be pleased.*

Father Rafael began. Alex closed his eyes and tried to sense his mother's presence in the room. He smelled the faint scent of the roses in front of him, but sensed nothing of her. He felt unsettled. She wasn't here. Alex struggled to listen to Father Rafael's homily, but heard only platitudes. *She's in a better place.* And where exactly was that? How did he accept her death when her body had never been recovered? He felt no comfort from the priest's words and stopped listening. Alex heard his name and fought back to the present.

"Alejandro, would you like to say a few words?"

Alex stood and turned to the assemblage. "My mom was the best mom, an incredible…." He stopped and cleared his throat. "You know my mom. She would be surprised by the number of people here…and worried that there wouldn't be enough food for you all. There will be. Please come back to the house afterward. Thank you for coming today. It means a lot to me."

"Thank you, Alejandro." Father Rafael said. "At this time, anyone who wishes, please come forward and share memories of Rosaria."

After an initial hesitation, a line formed along the wall.

"My name is Juanita Arreola. Rosaria was my best friend since elementary school. We married at the same time, and had our first children almost the same day. Alejandro was born April 30; my Carlos was born May 3. We raised our babies together. There was not one day when we didn't talk— in person or on the phone. Then we each bought our first houses. Rosaria stayed here in East Los Angeles. I moved to Fresno. Neither of us could afford to travel to see each other, but we kept in touch by letters. I saved each one Rosaria wrote to me." She held up a bulging tote. "Alejandro, these are for you. Every letter is about you…of you growing up. She loved you so much. I hope her words will comfort you."

Alex stood and embraced her. He clutched the package of letters to his chest and returned to his seat.

"I'm recording this," Judith whispered. She pointed to her cell phone.

Alex bit his lip and nodded. The next speaker came to the podium.

"I know Rosaria long time. She live—¿comó se dice?—al lado de mí?" The middle-aged man's snaky gnarled hands gripped the podium.

"Next door to me!" a female voice called out.

"Sí. Next. Door. To. Me. Rosaria she say, 'Pablo, you smart guy. Go to school in night. Learn English. Get good job.' You know Rosaria. I do what Rosaria say." He shook his finger in the air. People chuckled. "Today I Head Groundskeeper at Marriott Hotel."

He opened his jacket and pointed to a plastic name tag affixed to his shirt. "Alejandro, your mother is good woman. She care. Vaya con Dios." He tipped his head to Alex.

After Alex shook the last hand and returned the last hug, he slumped with exhaustion, but felt better than he had in a long, long time. He would sleep tonight.

Now his mother could rest in peace, too.

Chapter 16

Until the day her letter arrived.
Mexican stamps. Postmarked last week. No return address. *She was well. She was happy. She would write again.*

Chapter 17

When the doctor finally arrived, Julio tried to keep him from entering.

"I know this one," Doctor Goméz said. "Out of the way, boy."

Julio turned and disappeared.

Later, after the doctor's diagnosis of pneumonia, he marshaled male neighbors to carry Pajarito, strapped onto a gurney, to his clinic.

After a week of potent intravenous antibiotics and nutrition, Pajarito rallied, weak, but among the living.

"She can leave here, but she still needs care. She's too feeble to be alone, and she can't count on that drunkard of a grandson to help her," Doctor Goméz said.

"She can stay with me," Rosaria said.

"She's going to need a lot of care. How will you manage?" Doctor Goméz looked down at Rosaria, a foot shorter than he and many pounds lighter.

Rosaria put her hands on her hips and lifted her chin. "I'm stronger than I look," she said.

"I'm sure you are."

"And I'm sure you can recommend someone who would

stay with us to help until Pajarito's back on her feet. I'll pay her well," Rosaria said.

"Your home is beautiful, Rosita," Pajarito said. She leaned on her cane as she gazed around Rosaria's living room at the gleaming wood floor, the carved sofa, and the matching chairs covered with bright blue and purple fabrics.

"Daniela, come here to meet Pajarito," Rosaria called.

A young woman wiping her hands on her apron approached the women. "Tengo mucho gusto, señora," she said in a soft voice. She half curtseyed.

"Daniela is a wonderful help to me, and the best cook. She will make us fat. Come. See your room, Pajarito."

She led her friend down the hall to Mamá and Papá's bedroom. Rosaria knew they remembered Pajarito, her little friend who had scampered in the yard with her until darkness enveloped them. *Thank you, Mamá and Papá, for welcoming Parjarito and embracing her with your healing love.*

"Gracias, mi amiga Rosíta," Pajarito said, as she patted the white bedspread embroidered with tropical flowers. After Pajarito nestled herself like a tiny queen in a palace of pillows, Rosaria slipped her friend's shoes off and covered her with a woven afghan.

"¿Dónde está Julio?" Pajarito asked.

"No sé."

Rosaria knew. Everyone knew where Julio was. He spent his days in an alcohol fueled stupor. Whatever money

Pajarito had hidden in her home vanished into the gut of her grandson. When the money ran out, Rosaria expected him on her doorsep. Until then, Pajarito gained strength. She would need it.

Party time. Inside Rosaria's home, people holding plates stacked high with black beans, tamales, chile verde, picadillo, and poc-chuc conversed and gestured between bites. Their voices rose in volume as more guests arrived. Children dashed among the adults and laughed at anyone trying to corral them. Her back yard held the overflow, about another couple dozen or so. *Where had all these people come from?* Invited guests brought family members, extended family members, neighbors, people they met along the way, anyone and everyone, all invited. That was the Mexican way. A party meant all were welcome. Rosaria's *Welcome Home to Me* party had grown into the event of the year.

At first Rosaria worried about feeding the multitudes. However, as each guest arrived carrying casseroles of enchiladas, chile Colorado, pibil pollo, chilorio, and Spanish rice, Rosaria's concerns turned to where to put all the contributions. Smells of salsa picante, garlic, and cooking oil drifted from kitchen. Daniela had prepared huge kettles of menudo, vats of refried beans, dishes of chunky guacamole, flour and corn tortillas and savory traditional breads. For dessert. she created creamy flan, pastel de tres leches, and capirotada. The kitchen table and counter tops overflowed. Not to worry. Men grabbed leftover pieces of lumber and laid them over cast-off saw benches. Instant tables sprang up, smaller ones in the house, and larger ones in the back yard.

No ghosts present today, unless they put in their ear plugs. When Rosaria saw the number of musicians, five, and heard their volume, loud, she set them up on the porch. As these men blew their horns, their neck veins pulsed and bulged. Until Dr. Gómez arrived, Rosaria hoped someone else knew CPR. When he walked up the porch steps, holding out a bottle of wine, Rosaria greeted him with gusto. Her emergency medical responder was on the premises.

At the far end of the porch, several couples danced, and little children jumped up and down surrounding them, as they batted at the lower hanging balloons. One small boy grabbed the end of a blue crepe paper streamer and twirled until he transformed himself into a miniature blue mummy.

As Rosaria moved through the clusters of people, a man stepped in front of her. Although his face was weather worn, he stood erect, so tall that his head nearly brushed the string of lights hanging from the olive tree.

"Great party," he said.

"Have we met?" she said.

"We drank. We danced." He raised his beer bottle to her.

The cantina her first night in town, all that dizzy whirling and the strong arms holding her. How many times had she returned to read the entry in her journal? But his face had eluded her, and here he stood. And he was *handsome*.

"I'm Mario," he said, extending his hand and closing it over hers. He kept it there. Her face warmed, and the warmth spread to her body.

"Thank you for coming." She pulled her hand free and moved to walk past him.

"Save a dance for me," he said. He touched her arm as she passed.

Rosaria went into Mamá and Papá's bedroom, where Ynez sat propped up by multiple pillows. A brilliant serape cradled her shoulders. Some women guests had pulled chairs into the room to gossip.

"Come. We are talking about everyone who isn't in this room," one woman named Eliazar said. She had been a tough girl at school, the one who threw pebbles at their backs as she and Ynez ran home. "Run, you scared little girls," she had taunted. Age had mellowed her somewhat. She no longer threw stones, but her tongue retained its sharpness.

"I must talk to everyone," Rosaria said.

Groups of chatting guests slid out of their way as she and Diablo moved through the house to the front door. As they emerged onto the porch, the horns stumbled in mid-blast for a few off-key seconds, and then resumed their boisterous tune. Rosaria led Diablo down the porch steps and looked back at her parents' house, her home. The wind chime, made from discarded liquor bottles tossed into her yard at night, hung from a porch beam and flashed bright reflections of light. The clinking of the bottles in the breeze reminded her to be brave, whenever she felt apprehensive. *Thank you, God, for your protection—and for bringing me here, to this glorious day.*

Tequila, in moderation, if there was such a thing, left her feeling a pleasant malaise. Pleasant Oaks should have served it in the dining room. She laughed out loud at the thought of all those old people chugging down tequila shots, their muted conversations exploding into shouting.

Above the loud music, a male voice screamed; and loud growls rumbled from her left. She hurried in that direction and pushed through her gate. Tall plants whacked her face as she pressed forward until she saw Diablo, his jaws clamped onto the pants cuff of a struggling man, who kicked and twisted. The cuff ripped free from the garment, until only inches held it to the pants leg.

"Diablo! Drop!" Rosaria said.

After one final snarl, he dropped the fabric. He stood at alert, watching the man. The man lurched, balanced, and turned to Rosaria.

"You bitch," he said.

"Julio!" Rosaria stepped back and fell. The low growth cushioned her fall, leaving her bones intact, but her dignity wounded. Julio advanced. Diablo sprang at him and knocked him to the ground and locked his teeth over Julio's right arm. Rosaria rolled to her stomach, got to her knees and grabbed a bush branch to pull herself upright.

"Get your devil dog off me," Julio said.

"Good boy, Diablo," she said.

Diablo's head tossed back and forth as he held on.

"Call him off."

"You're making it worse. Keep still."

"Get off me, stupid dog," he said. He kicked a foot at Diablo. Diablo bit down, hard. Julio shrieked and lay still. Rosaria grabbed Diablo's collar.

"Drop, boy," she said. When he didn't obey, she said, "Drop! Now!"

Julio rolled into a fetal position and cradled his arm to his chest. "I'm bleeding."

"Come with me. Dr. Sanchez is at my house."

"I'm not going anywhere with you."

"Oh, yes you are."

Julio weaved ahead of them toward her home. When Julio paused, Diablo warned him with low rumbles. Rosaria herself could have tracked Julio, blindfolded, by the stink of him. Urine, sweat, and alcohol wafted in a putrid cloud behind him. Rosaria brought her cotton handkerchief to her nose and kept it there. So this is what had become of Julio—more of the same, only worse.

As Julio, Diablo, and Rosaria broke out onto the path and approached her gate, a dancing couple gawked at them from the porch. Rosaria waved, and they returned their attention to each other and their dancing. Rosaria walked around her fence to the back yard. Clusters of men stood close to coolers stuffed with bottles. She opened the back gate and moved to a cooler, taking a beer from it. She brought it to Julio.

"Salud, Julio," she said. "Welcome to my home."

He sneered as he grabbed the bottle, snapped off the cap, and tipped it high. As he drank, Rosaria approached a trio of hefty young men standing nearby.

"Hola, señores," she said. "Watch Julio, please. Keep him in the back yard. Let him drink all he wants, and come tell me when he passes out."

As an insurance policy, she placed Diablo at the back

gate. "Stay, Diablo," she said. Diablo sat at attention, like a regal sentry. *No one is leaving my party early.*

Within an hour, one of the young guards came to her in the living room.

"Señora, he is out cold," he said. "Shall we throw him outside the gate to sleep it off?"

"No, leave him where he is, but turn him on his side. I'll bring Dr. Goméz out to check him out."

As the last of the revelers left, Dr. Goméz directed four men as they carried Julio between them, each supporting an appendage. The doctor had treated Julio's wound with an antiseptic and wrapped it in bandages, sufficient until he could minister to him in his office. He assured Rosaria that only a few stitches would be necessary. Julio's pockets yielded enough for his treatment. In the meantime, Rosaria would scour Pajarito's home and gather whatever money Julio hadn't found.

The next day, Rosaria hurried to the doctor with a bag of cash. "Here, enough for his rehab," she said.

"Rehab? Rosaria, you're not in California anymore," Dr. Goméz replied.

"Where do people here go?"

He pointed out his window. "They usually end up over there…in the jail…where they sober up, get out, and do it all over again."

"Keep him here with you, until you're sure he won't have seizures."

"And then?"

"And then…." Rosaria pointed across the street to the jail.

"Rosaria, he'll go right back to drinking once he's out. They all do."

"Doctor, do you know anyone who didn't?"

"Only one."

An interior door to the row of cells opened and Caesar, the jailer, led Rosaria into the corridor. Caesar's tassled golden shoulder epaulets flipped as he walked.

Julio gripped the bars. Two weeks without a drink, and alcohol still leeched from him, filling the confined space with its sour smell.

"Let me out of here!"

"Stop, señor," the officer said.

"Hello, Julio," Rosaria said.

"Come closer, old woman."

"I'll speak to you from right here."

"I didn't do anything wrong. You have no right to keep me here."

"Please," Rosaria said, drawing out the word. "This is Mexico."

"Sí, es México," Caesar said. He held up the ring of keys and jingled them.

Another man entered the hallway, his boots click-clicking

on the tiled floor, and walked up to the cell door. He removed his cowboy hat and smoothed his long dark hair back from his forehead.

"Hello, Julio," he said.

"You look familiar. You my attorney?" Julio said.

"You've watched too much television," Caesar said.

Caesar inserted the key, and swung the door open. "Be my guest."

The man entered and swung the heavy door shut behind him. "Now lock us in and leave. We need privacy."

With a glance over her shoulder, Rosaria followed Caesar to the front office.

"You sure he'll be safe?" Rosaria asked.

"Which one? Javiar knows how to handle himself. Don't worry about him. Julio's in for a big surprise when he finds out who Javiar really is," the officer said.

Chapter 18

Diablo stretched, his nails scratching along the wooden planks. Smells of coffee and frying chilies drifted under Rosaria's bedroom door. To her surprise, she had acclimated to the daily infusion of hot peppers into every meal. The ability to digest spicy foods must be genetic, she decided. At regular intervals, Daniela brought home long strings of bright red peppers from the outdoor market. What Rosaria thought would take them a year to eat, they finished in two weeks.

Rosaria slid into her woven slippers and padded down the hall to the bathroom. She hoped God didn't mind that she kept her Bible there. Every time she sat on the toilet—and she sat there often, day and night—she opened the Bible to a random page and read. Most times, she read a useful passage. If she chose a page past the middle, she was more likely to get the message she needed. The front part, the Old Testament, was far too gloomy. The New Testament spoke to her new life.

Where would she be today if she hadn't left? She saw herself back in the Great Room at Shady Oaks. Great because it was large, not because anything of merit occurred there. Occasional entertainment: pianists with arthritic knuckles who pounded out not-so-golden oldies, magicians in wrinkled black tuxes who produced stuffed rabbits, vocalists who thought volume substituted for pitch…. The list went on. The best thing that could be said was that these well-meaning people broke the monotony of the place. Same meals with the same people at the same table in the same dining room. In a few months, Rosie lost her appetite for food, and, in time, for living. Change only came when someone passed away—no one ever died at Shady Oaks—and a different person sat at her table. She began to believe the messages that were thrust at her every day. She became what others saw: a dried-up old woman of no practical use, sentenced to spend her remaining days confined with others of her ilk.

What if Alex found her, deemed her incompetent, and dragged her back to that wretched half life? Alex will not believe I was dying in that place. Here, I'm not dying; I'm living. *I will never go back. I will not.* Rosaria shook her head at the horror of her thoughts. That was then; this is now.

She opened her Bible to Psalms, always a good choice, and read from Chapter 92: *They still bear fruit in old age; they are ever full of sap and green….*

She liked that.

Rosaria turned over the soil around some succulents.

"Hola, Rosita. How are you…ahora?"

She waved her trowel at Pajarito, who stood on the porch.

By now, Rosaria was accustomed to their conversations of mixed-up Spanish and English.

"Hello, Pajarito. I am well today. How are you?" Rosaria replied, speaking with deliberate enunciation.

Pajarito put her hand on her lower back. "Hurt like… shit," she said. "Lo síento, I say shit."

"Shit is the right word. You hurt. That is shit. Talk to me while I work."

Pajarito lowered herself to a cushioned rocking chair and sighed. "Es good." She smiled down at Rosaria. "No es shit."

That night, Rosaria began her nightly journal entry with the title, *No Es Shit*. That summed up her life here. Back in California—she no longer thought of it as back home—she struggled each evening to write words of gratitude. Instead, words of anger and pain poured from her; words that she never wanted another living being to read, certainly not Alex. She had stabbed at the page with her pen as she wrote about her ghost-like existence at Shady Oaks. She had been Rosie in Room 103, nothing more, and lots less. No privacy, not even in the bathroom. The employees had master keys, and burst in, after a perfunctory knock, with fresh towels, or pills, or whatever. They seemed to think the need for modesty vanished as one aged.

Those old journals lay torn up and rotting in a California landfill.

Here—home in Mexico—grateful words flowed, and

she wrote in her new journal until her hand cramped. So much to tell. She flexed her writing hand, flipped pages back to earlier entries. Ah, here was one she had read several times before, '*Welcome Home to Me*' *Party*. As physically tired as she was that night, her mind whirled at bedtime. She had brought out her journal and written, from start to finish, every person, every conversation, and every observation of that night. Spanish and English words spilled from mind to pen, without conscious thought on her part.

Tonight, as she re-read that evening's entry, she came to the passage she particularly savored, her meeting with Mario. He had asked her to dance, and they never had. Why not? She'd been busy, flitting around to speak to her guests; and then there was that mess with Julio. *How old is Mario? He looked younger than me. Men my age are stooped and slow. Mario isn't. He's the opposite...erect and quick.* She waved her hand to cool her face. *Behave yourself, Rosaria.* She must have said it out loud, because Diablo got up and put his head on her knee.

She returned to the current day's writing. *Call Adriana tomorrow. Ask her to let me know the next time Mario comes to La Cantina.*

Rosaria's sessions of reading, formerly held at Ynez's sales cart, now took place on Rosaria's front porch. People brought their own chairs, or sat on the wooden floor. These crowds were testing its strength. Rosaria was glad her workmen had used thick planks, laid over concrete supports. When her porch was full, people sat on the steps, and squatted on the narrow lawn she nurtured just off the porch. Rosaria sat on a high barstool in her doorway, with Diablo at her feet.

Each day, Rosaria began her reading with an English lesson. She didn't call them that. She didn't want to scare off her audience. With Adriana's help, Rosaria ordered large print children's books, written in English, with colorful illustrations. After she read each page, she held the print high and turned it in all directions for everyone to see. Some of the women began to ask to borrow the books, to read to their children and grandchildren; and Rosaria handed them over with a smile.

In addition, when she read the adult books to them in Spanish, she began to sneak in some questions in English.

"Who is your favorite character? Favor de hablar en inglés," she told them.

No one was brave enough to answer in English. At last, a man in the back raised his hand. He stood at the far edge of the crowd each day, and gazed out over the yard as she read.

She hadn't thought he heard a word. She braced for his answer.

"Me...gusta Simone. Es hot mamá," he said. Women near her covered their mouths and tittered. The men threw back their head and roared. Rosaria waited for them to quiet.

"Yes, I like Simone, too. She is a hot mamá," Rosaria replied, smiling.

On impulse, she pulled a hard candy out of her pocket and tossed it high to him. He caught the candy and held it up to show the crowd.

Each time Adriana arrived at her door, Rosaria hoped for news about Mario, but her conversations were about new books that had arrived, and about bits of gossip she had overheard in the cantina. Several weeks later, after Pajarito had retired for the night, early sleeper that she was, Rosaria sat on the porch watching the sun meet the horizon. The muted yellow light made her garden glow like a sepia photograph.

Someone with a flashlight appeared at her gate, an out-of-breath Adriana.

"Señora Rosaria, he is at the cantina!"

"Mario?"

"Of course, Mario! I cannot wait for you. Come quickly. You need to get yourself a cell phone."

Rosaria got out the outfit she had chosen weeks before.

As she and Diablo walked through the darkness, Rosaria beamed a flashlight onto the path. The moon and stars lit the sky. In California, the stars had disappeared behind the pervasive street lights, her room at Shady Oaks never completely dark. She had existed under daytime fluorescent lights and half-slept in half-lit nighttime gloom. In Mexico, the stars shone in their pristine glory, like the sparkling white jewels God meant them to be. Night-time smells of jungle growth and blossoms perfumed the breezes from the sea. Her steps landed stable and sure, all her anxiety about what she was doing left behind, discarded on the trail. Diablo thumped his tail against her leg, letting her know he was enjoying this unusual nighttime walk—and at a faster pace than normal. This was fun. Rosaria thought so, too.

She heard the cantina before she saw it. Loud horns blared an exuberant tune that dared anyone within earshot to resist the pounding rhythms. She picked up her pace, and pulled Diablo along. He leaped and barked. Her full skirt, embroidered with bright tropical flowers, billowed around her. They hurried into the small village, past the Virgin fountain. No water dripped. Mary had nights off to rest from her perpetual daytime sorrows. At the bottom of the steps to the cantina, Rosaria grabbed for the banister; and her foot caught as she attempted the first step. She plopped down on the bottom dusty wooden step and struggled to breathe normally.

"Señora Rosaria, are you well?" A male voice called from the dark porch.

Mario stood, backlit from the cantina's interior lights, handsome as a cover shot from one of the books she read aloud to her front porch audiences.

"I'm fine."

"Here. Let me help you." He hurried to the step above her, and extended his hand. She reached out, and felt his broad hand close over hers as he helped her up the steps.

Where was Diablo? He stood at the bottom of the steps, his head cocked as if to say, *Now what?* Adriana would bring out a water dish for him...and some bits of leftover food.

"Let me buy you a drink," Mario said. "You can repay me with a dance."

Rosaria could not summon one word…of English nor Spanish.

As they danced, she remembered the pressure of his hand on her back and his sure grip of her right hand, as he led her around the room to the beat of the music. Tonight, unclouded by the fog of too much liquor, she knew she would remember every moment.

"You are one dancing lady," Mario said, as he pulled out her chair for her. He sat down, untied the red kerchief from his neck, and wiped his forehead.

"And you are one dancing hombre."

"We need another drink…before we dance again." He raised his hand to summon Adriana. "And I do like that bright green blouse you're wearing, señora."

"Please call me Rosaria."

Chapter 19

Cappi Caporali, Private Investigator, the painted letters on the door stated. The tough-guy Italian name appealed to him. *Maybe I should have called ahead. He might be too busy to see me, or not in.* He need not have worried. After he knocked, an affirmative grunt came from within. Alex pulled open the door and entered a cubicle, large enough to accommodate a small metal desk and the big man who sat behind it. If the door had opened inward, it would have bumped the furniture. An empty chair was wedged into the left corner. Alex found himself wondering how the man got behind the desk. From the size of the room, he'd have to crawl over or under it. Alex found the answer when the man sucked in his gut, and—graceful as a ballerina—side-stepped between his desk and the wall.

"Cappi Caporali. Call me Cap. Pleased to meet you." His voice matched his girth. "What can I do for you, Mr...?"

"Alex Rodríguez."

He pointed to the metal chair. By the time Alex seated himself, Cap Caporali sat behind his desk again. The man was nothing if not agile. That might be important for someone in his line of work, Alex decided, his certainty based on the television shows and movies he had seen.

"I need you to find my mother," Alex began. He handed him his mother's letter.

Half an hour later, Alex had ended his story. Just the telling had relieved his anxiety. The tenseness left his shoulders, and the knot in his stomach untied itself.

Caporali leaned forward. "What I find may not be what you want. Your mother may not want to be found."

"I need to know. I'm going crazy."

"No guarantees. Her trail is cold. Let's see what I can come up with in a week. I'll send you email updates and call you every night at eight."

Alex felt hopeful for the first time in months. As he stood up to leave, he resisted the urge to reach over the desk and hug Cap Caporali.

Wait until I tell Judith! He rethought that idea until it morphed into: *Wait. Don't tell Judith yet.* He would disguise Cap's retainer as a business expense for awhile.

True to his promise, Cap called the next evening.

"Did you know your mother had another bank account at the Bank of Southern California?"

"You sure?"

"She took out every penny in that account—$237,000 and change."

Alex tried to analyze Cap's words, but his brain was on overload. "Why didn't my attorney find this out? He's supposed to be settling her estate."

"I'm sure he would have, in time. Listen, the bank manager has a policy of speaking personally with anyone who withdraws a large amount, especially an elderly customer. The manager said your mother was unaccompanied and she was very poised, said she was going to invest the money elsewhere. She demanded $5,000 in cash, despite the manager's protests, and the balance in a cashier's check. Alex, she basically took off with the money stuffed into her shopping bag," he said.

"That woman wasn't my mom."

"It was your mom. The bank manager ID'd the photo I showed him. It was definitely her."

"I can't believe this."

"Think. She planned this. Where would she go? In the meantime, I'll check the airlines, the trains, the buses. She paid cash, but someone will remember her, an old lady traveling alone. And from what you tell me about her, she'd interact with others."

"I can't think straight right now. I'll call you back. She's in danger, Cap, carrying all that money. You got to find her."

"I'm on it."

Chapter 20

Although it was impossible, she swore she could still smell Mario's cologne. As soon as she opened the front door a few inches, Diablo pushed it wide and ran out into the front yard. Rosaria reached high, breathed in the fresh morning air, and stretched on tip toe.

"Hello, Beautiful," Mario said.

She spun toward the living room and his voice.

"Oh," she said. She crossed her arms across her breasts, which felt exposed beneath her cotton nightgown.

Mario pushed himself up on an elbow from his prone position on the couch…her couch. He threw back the quilt, revealing his bare chest.

Good Lord, I hope he has something on down below. Her mind said look away, but her eyes stayed locked on him.

"I thought you'd left," Rosaria said.

"You wore me out last night," he said. "You sure can dance. Too tired to drive home, so I bedded down here. Sorry if I scared you."

Daniela hurried about the kitchen preparing their breakfast, all the while sneaking looks at them at the table. Eggs, onions, and jalapenos sizzled on the stove, their fragrance filling the room.

Diablo stretched out on the tile floor beneath the table. *Some guard dog. Didn't even warn me about a man in my own living room, nor object to him at my kitchen table.* Quite the opposite. Diablo devoured the tortilla pieces that Mario tore off and slipped under the table to him.

Daniela set a steaming plate of food in front of Mario.

"Good cook," he said.

Daniela giggled and whirled back to the stove.

I'm the only one keeping my wits about me in this kitchen.

"Hola, Rosita. And hola to you, Mario," Pajarito said from the doorway.

Rosario yanked up the neckline of the cotton robe she had grabbed from the back of her armoire.

"Sit down and eat," Rosario said.

By the end of a month, Mario's morning visits no longer surprised them. Diablo no longer barked, Daniela left the kitchen door unlocked, and Rosaria dressed before breakfast. Mario announced his arrival to them with the clumping of his big feet on the rug outside and a knock. He burst in, carrying papáyas, mangos, or flowers—his contributions to their meals together.

"He must have much new business in town," Pajarito said, giving Rosaria a long look.

At least once a week, he returned to Rosaria's casa before dark and took her to the cantina.

Rosaria's audience had arrived today and hurried to claim a spot, preferably somewhere shaded by plants or roof. It was early December, but you wouldn't know by the temperature. People crowded onto Rosaria's porch and spilled onto her front yard. She peered out her front window and did a head count. Thirty-one. Could that be? The mornings Mario came for breakfast, he stayed on for her readings. He stood at the edge of the group, his feet wide and his arms folded, as if marking his territory. With his attendance, had come a marked increase in her listeners. She knew why.

Two women in porch chairs leaned close.

"And how do you suppose the handsome Señor Mario is feeling this fine morning?"

"Muy, muy bien. I hear he likes to read, too."

One woman slapped the other on her arm, and they hooted with laughter. When they saw Rosaria, they quieted and sat up straight.

Her real-life romance, if she dared call it that, piqued everyone's interest more than the romance novels she read to them. How would her story turn out? If the crowd kept growing, soon she would need a microphone. She inhaled, exhaled, opened her front door, regarded the two gossiping women, and took her place on the stool.

Perched on the railing to her left, Julio tipped his San Diego Padres baseball cap her way. Pajarito's grandson, sober for six months, made his amends to his grandmother with long visits, and his amends to Rosaria with yard work. She paid him fair wages for his efforts, including his time on her porch listening to her read.

She raised her book and began.

After the last person drifted away out her gate, Mario stacked the plastic chairs along the front wall of her porch. His task completed, he stood next to her. He leaned close. "You are a powerful reader. Much emotion. I saw your tears when Susanna's lover left her."

Rosaria reached up and swiped at her cheeks. "All part of the act," she said.

"And this?" he asked. He cupped her face in his hands and kissed her.

She put her hands on top of his and kissed him back. She was beginning to feel like a wanton, bosom-buster of a woman, just like in her books; and she liked the feeling.

"So, Señora Rosaria, what're we going to do about us?" he asked.

Rosaria requested an appointment with Father Antonio in his office. Rosaria had a question, and she wanted to see his eyes when he answered. Today, the darkness of the confessional wouldn't do. She needed light.

"How may I help you?"

To Rosaria, he looked like an altar boy playing dress-up

in priest's garb. His efforts to appear older, growing a beard, compounded his youthfulness. He looked like an altar boy dressed like a priest and wearing pasted-on facial hair. She almost convinced herself that if she gave his beard a tug, it would come off.

"Father, I'm thinking about entering into a relationship with a man," she said.

"Oh?" he said.

"Not living with him. But…"

"What are asking me, Rosaria?"

"I'm asking…whether it's a sin, in the eyes of God."

The priest wagged his index finger at her, but his eyes warmed. "You know the answer to that already, Rosaria. God sees the total person. He sees the many kindnesses you've shown your friends, and all the good you've done. Your generosity counts in God's eyes."

"What about Mario?" She put her hand to her mouth. She hadn't meant to say his name.

"Ah, yes, Mario." Rosaria recognized the affirmation of his name, not the astonishment she had expected. "Come to the confessional anytime you need to…and as often as you need to."

Chapter 21

"He remembers her, Alex," Cap said. "The cop at the downtown bus station says she rolled her suitcase right over his feet. Then told him later 'the ladies' room needs looking after,' her exact words to him."

"How'd you trace her there?" Alex asked.

"I checked out the taxi pickups near Shady Oaks that night. The guy who picked her up remembered her—an old lady humming a song throughout the ride, he told me. Made one stop before the bus depot. Guess where?" Cap didn't stop for a breath or for an answer. "At your mother's house. Had him wait. Said she went around the back of the house for ten minutes on his meter. Had a plastic bag with her, and didn't have it when she got back in the cab."

"What was in the bag?"

"Looked like some clothing to him."

"So, she's on the way to catch a bus and stops to dump her clothing into the ditch behind our old house? Why?"

"First thing I plan to ask her. Cabbie said he was worried about dropping her off so late downtown, not the best area."

"So, why did he?"

"Says she told him she'd be fine, she was meeting her son

in the bus station. So, he drops her off, right at the door, and watches her walk in."

"Then what?"

"I checked with the ticket seller on duty that night. He wasn't sure he saw her, says he sells tickets to 'lots of old farts,' not the most PC guy. I waited until he went out for a smoke break and brought him around to more enlightened thinking…convinced him this particular old fart was really special to her son. This is why I don't go on a diet." Cap patted his belly.

Alex waved his hand in a go-on motion.

"Says she bought a ticket to Mexico, to a place called Flores Bonitas. Ever heard of it?"

"Heard of it? That's where Mom was born. I should have thought of that before. But she spent her life trying to rid herself of that place. I've been wasting my time looking for her here, and she went back to *that*? She must have lost it."

"Wait, Alex. Listen to the rest. She's not there."

"So, where is she?"

"Sorry to give this to you so piecemeal, but that's the way my mind works, chronologically."

"Skip to the end, Cap."

"The bus driver says he remembers her really well. She 'created problems,' he said. Kept getting up and yelling for stuff for a baby."

"What baby?"

"Apparently your mother sat with a young woman who had a baby with her. Your mom, the mother, and baby got off at the first stop across the border. Not really a town, just a village. Some place called El Alto."

"Is that a joke? That means 'The Stop' in English. Why would she get off there? Flores Bonitas is a couple hundred or more miles south, on the east coast."

"Driver says he overheard talk of taking the baby to a doctor."

"How's my mother involved?" Alex waved his hand dismissively before Cap could respond. "Hey, it doesn't matter. I'm going down there and bring her back. She's obviously not functioning very well."

"Slow down. Let's talk about this, Alex."

"What's to talk about? I know where she is, and I'm going to go get her."

"Alex, think about it. She crossed the border a long, long time ago."

"If she's not in El Alto anymore, people will have talked to her and know where she's went from there, probably to Flores Bonitas. I'll start with finding the doctor. I'm going."

"You speak Spanish?"

"Enough to get by. Mom made me speak English, always—didn't want me to 'sound like a Mexican'—but I picked up a lot, despite her. In fact, my neighborhood buddies taught me a few choice words."

"Alex, I'm going with you. Mexico's a dangerous place these days, especially in the border towns."

At first, Alex wanted to take the same bus his mother had taken. He wanted to talk to the driver himself. Cap convinced him the bus would take so much longer, and that nothing more could be learned from the driver. When they loaded up Alex's truck for the trip, Alex recognized the most compelling reason for private transportation. Cap's jacket flared open as he fastened the seatbelt around his ample middle, and Alex saw the gun in its holster.

Alex returned to the house and came back with his hunting rifle. He slid it into the space beneath the truck's bench seat.

Chapter 22

"Last exit before the Mexican Border" the freeway sign-post indicated. Alex squinted into the late night fog. To the right, a motel light blinked a red welcome—or warning. "Motel," no pretense. He exited. As he drove closer, a low stretch of a stucco building came into view. A few vehicles were scattered here and there in front. The office glowed with a dim yellow light, like an old-fashioned bug lamp. No AAA rating. No problem. Alex could afford to reserve two rooms, instead of one, at this fine establishment and get it on one bill, for Judith's careful records.

Alex cut off his engine. Cap continued to slump and snore, both hands clutching nearly empty bags of chips. More crumbled bags littered the floorboard and covered his feet. The entire drive had been punctuated by the steady rhythm of Cap's chewing. He even ate while he talked. Alex imagined trying to Heimlich the large man if he choked. His arms would never reach around that middle.

From the appearance of the skinny guy behind the motel counter, he'd been asked to do far more illicit activities than doctor a bill—like bury bodies in the adjacent sand dunes. He wore crooked, heavily framed black glasses, one lens obscured by grease streaks, the other by solid duct tape. When he bent down to scribble the receipt, Alex leaned forward. Did this guy have an eye behind that tape? Yellow and blue discolorations flared beyond the white medical tape. Alex tried to imagine the punch, through the guy's glasses, the splintering glass piercing his eye.

"Your eye going to be okay?" Alex asked.

"Sure, no problem. Damn those door knobs." He handed Alex the metal keys, no keycards at this place, and the receipt. "Last rooms, at the back, so you won't be disturbed." He pointed to the hourly rate posted behind him. "Unless...."

"No thanks, we're good."

Cap roused himself as Alex eased the truck into a slot in front of their rooms.

"What the? This the Bates Motel?"

"Even better," Alex replied. "It's got room service." He pointed back to the small lettering beneath the generic "Motel." *Hourly Rates* flashed in blush red. "Didn't see it when I pulled in, but, hey, you're a single guy." He jabbed at Cap's arm.

"Yeah, right. That'd give me a life-time souvenir to take home. You're quite the funny guy." He punched Alex's arm in return. Alex stopped himself from rubbing away the pain.

Alex stretched out, fully clothed, on top of a blanket he had brought in from his truck. Who knew what tales these bedspreads could tell? Alex swore he wouldn't be able to sleep, not with the constant coming and going of noisy vehicles.

Couldn't these people afford mufflers? Well, if it came to a choice between a trip to a mechanic and a trip here…. He got up, pulled down a venetian blind slat and peered out. Couples weaved from their cars into the rooms, no stop at the office required. Wonder how much Motel guy charged them for an hour. At the rate people were coming and going, One Eye would be able to afford a cornea transplant in no time. Alex settled into his bed, counting customers and multiplying hours until sleep overtook him.

An exterior door exploded against a wall, and Alex bolted awake and out of bed. He ran to open his door, remembered where he was, and stopped. He crept to the window. Was that Cap out there? In the faintly lit parking lot, Cap stood with his back to Alex. His revolver extended out in his right hand, and he clasped the hand of a short woman in the other. Three men stood in front on him, yelling and flinging their arms around. Cap began to move backwards, pulling the woman with him, and sweeping his gun back and forth at the men.

"¡Alto! ¡Alto!" Cap shouted and gestured with his gun. "Alto, I, said!" The men crept forward and widened the distance between themselves. In seconds, Cap wouldn't be able to keep his gun on all of them. Alex grabbed his rifle and opened the door.

"¡Buenas noches, amigos! ¿Qué pasa?" Alex brought his rifle up and clicked the chamber.

"Good to hear your voice, amigo," Cap said, "and your fire power." He kept his eyes on the advancing men.

"Abajo en el suelo," Alex said.

Three pairs of knees hit the dirt. The woman started to kneel, but Cap jerked her upright.

"What I've been telling them."

"Cap, they don't understand English."

"I thought I spoke their language." He brandished his weapon.

"What's going on, Cap?" Alex pointed to the back of the woman.

Cap twirled her around to face Alex. A young girl, maybe 13, if that, clasped her free hand over her torn blouse and shivered. Her eyes stayed on her bare feet.

"These guys thought they'd save some money, split the hourly rate. Three guys, one room, and one little girl. Heard her screaming…." Cap shrugged as if to say this was all the explanation necessary.

Alex bent over the men. "¡Fuera de aqui! ¡Vayase! ¡Ahora!"

The men struggled to their feet.

"What? No way I'm letting these scumballs go. I'm calling 911," Cap said.

"Not a good idea. How can this place operate without the cops knowing about it?"

Cap kept his gun trained on the men, who craned their heads forward, trying to understand. "Ok, but tell them that if they ever touch a little girl again, I'll track them down and cut off their balls."

"Mi amigo loco dice vaya con Dios," Alex said. The men exchanged looks. *Go with God?* Alex pointed his rifle barrel at the ground. "¡Vaya con Dios! Ahora!" he said, louder.

They scrambled to their feet and ran across the lot into the darkness.

Cap slapped Alex on the back. "That's why I need you, my amigo, to translate for me." Freed from Cap's hand, the girl stood and waited. "Ask her where she lives, Alex."

"No way, Cap. She's not our responsibility."

"She's a kid with torn clothing, bare feet. And those guys are still out there. If you don't want to call the police, fine. But I'm not leaving her here. Talk to her, Alex."

Alex bent over and touched the girl's dark head. She covered her eyes with her hands. Alex whispered. "¿Comó se llama usted?" Without movement, she whispered, "Verónica."

"Esta bien, Veronica. Esta bien. Donde esta su familia?

At his last words, she glanced up at him, her eyes a mixture of fear and bewilderment. "En México," she said.

So much for a peaceful night's sleep. The men slumped in stiff-backed chairs and took turns staying awake while Veronica slept on what had been Alex's bed. At dawn, they roused Veronica and set off. Cap, alert from his daytime naps and nighttime excitement, drove toward the border crossing. Alex dozed in the passenger seat, while Veronica slept the sleep of the exhausted, nestled in blankets on the narrow floor between the front and rear seats. Alex woke up when Cap took an exit before the border and pulled into a donut shop. Back on the freeway, Cap wolfed down some of the dozen donuts he bought, and passed the remainder to Alex.

In the morning haze, bright lights on high poles lit the

multiple lanes leading to the international border check. Cap eased into the shortest line. Alex covered their secret passenger's head with his jacket.

"Smuggling someone into Mexico. Bet this's a first." Cap slapped the steering wheel.

"Don't congratulate yourself until we're on the other side," Alex replied.

Alex slipped his hand back behind his bucket seat, resting it on Veronica's back, ready to hold her down if she started to get up. He felt her body rise and fall in the steady breathing of sleep. Good, let's hope she stays this way until they were across. A girl and guns. They would be in a mess of trouble if these border police were given any reason to search their vehicle.

Cap pulled forward and rolled down his window. "Howdy, officer, sir," Cap said. He smiled widely and lowered his head in the officer's direction.

"Your passports?" the officer said. He held out his hand. No return smile.

Cap handed over his and Alex's passports. "Here you go, sir," Cap said.

The officer scanned from their passports to their faces. "And what's the purpose of your visit?"

"My first trip, sir. Always wanted to see exotic Mexico. "

"Where, exactly, will you be traveling in Mexico?"

"Ah, to that Boney Floors place, sir. Oh, I forgot you say it backwards—Floors Boney—on the beach. You know it? Great fishing there, I hear. Want to catch something really big…and good to eat, of course." Cap patted his middle.

Without a word, the policeman returned their passports and waved them forward.

"See, piece of cake!" Cap said. He pumped his arm in the air.

Veronica's head popped up between them. "Sí, me gusta cake!" she said. Alex handed her a donut.

Amid squatting men, the faded metal signpost for El Alto sat in a dirt mound, just off the highway. Cap turned onto the unpaved road and slowed. The men swiveled to watch them pass. "There it is! This is where your mom got off." His face beamed.

"Yeah, yeah, Cap. I saw it," annoyed at Cap for stating the obvious, and for his enthusiasm for...everything. The truck bounced over the rock-strewn road. Over the crest of a hill and they were there, a huddle of small adobe buildings, with one larger white-washed building at the far end.

"Quite the bustling metropolis," Cap said.

Alex pointed. "There. That's got to be the doctor's place."

As Cap stopped the truck, dust flowed up and over it. "What do you call a doctor who graduates last in a Mexican medical school?"

"What?"

"El doctor in El Alto!" Cap cut the motor, and reached under the seat for his gun.

"Let's go see the good doctor."

"Cap, I'll do the talking."

"Of course, amigo. That's why I brought you along."

Alex motioned for Veronica to stay in the truck. She snugged down into the blankets and closed her eyes again.

Cap tapped on the door with his gun, then held it behind his back. Alex nudged Cap out of the way, slashing his hand across his mouth in a gesture meaning, shut up. In case Cap didn't get it, Alex said, "Not a word."

"My lips are sealed, good buddy." Cap twisted his lips with two fingers, and crooked his little finger. "Pinky swear, man."

"Cap, so help me—," The door swung open.

"¿Qué?" A tall man stood in the doorway, swaying a little, his legs in a wide stance.

"¿Usted el doctor? Alex asked.

"Sí, Sí," he said. "Qué quiere usted?" He spoke slowly and deliberately, the stink of alcohol wafting toward them with each syllable.

"Pretty early in the morning," Cap muttered.

Alex shot him a look.

Cap flashed his teeth and his left pinky.

"Dónde está mi madre?" Alex thrust a photo of his mother toward the doctor's face.

"¿Su madre? Shit," he said.

In a whirl of motion, Cap pivoted and shoved Alex out of the way. "I got the shit part," Cap said. He poked the doctor's chest with his gun. "Where is she, doctor shit-head?"

The doctor covered his face with his hands. "Please. Do not shoot me."

"Good. English. Where is she?" Cap grabbed the photo from Alex and waved it.

"She left." The doctor's fingers mimicked mini walking. "Rapido" he added, pointing towards the barren terrain behind his building.

"She ran…into the desert?" Cap asked.

"Why? Where was she going?" Alex said.

"I do not know. Lo siento. Es verdad." the doctor replied.

"Stop poking him with that gun, Cap. He doesn't know where she went."

"He sure knows why she ran."

The doctor hung his head to his chest and shrugged his shoulders.

"How long did she stay?" Cap asked.

"Three days."

Alex tugged on Cap's sleeve. "Enough, Cap. Let's check the map and see what the closest town is." As he turned to leave with Cap in tow, Alex stumbled into Veronica. How long had she been behind them?

"Hola, chica bonita," the doctor said. His red-rimmed eyes glowed. His tongue flicked across his lips. He stepped back and gestured for her to come in.

"Back off. She's with us," Cap said.

"That old woman is crazy!" The doctor held up a scarred left hand.

Chapter 23

"Give it up, Cap."

Cap pushed the truck's radio button…again. The screen remained blank, searching, searching, until it found a station. Guitars strummed, trumpets blared, and a guy sang like he was about to break into sobs.

After they left El Alto, the landscape didn't change. Desert, desert everywhere, and not a drop to drink. Even with the air on full blast, the cab was sweltering. Alex removed his Dodgers baseball cap and pulled his sticky shirt away from his chest. Damn, these polyester, no-iron shirts were hot. Shitty shirt. He liked the potential sound of it and tried it out loud. "Shitty shirt!" he said.

"Feel better now? Don't suppose we'll be coming to a Taco Bell?" Cap pulled off the red bandana he'd tied around his head, wiped his forehead, and twisted the bandana back into place. He looked like a gone-to-seed Hell's Angel. Might not be a bad look for a drive into Mexico.

"That's not real Mexican food."

"Mexican enough for me." Cap patted his belly and leaned down toward it. "Hear it?" He lowered his voice in his best imitation of a boxing ring announcer. "It's saying, 'Let's get ready to rumble!'"

"Don't see any place out here. Eat some of those snacks you bought at our last stop."

Cap picked up a fist full of empty bags. "All gone," he said.

"You're hopeless."

"No, I'm hopeful—that you'll find us some food, sooner rather than later." Cap turned to the space behind their seats. "Veronica, yo hungry? Es righto?"

Veronica popped up. "Sí, señor," she responded. She smiled broadly.

"See, how much Spanish I've picked up already," Cap said. He leaned back against his seat and crossed his arms.

Alex tipped down his sunglasses. "She answers 'sí' to whatever you say."

Up ahead, Alex saw a faded wooden sign: *Bebidas Frías*, with a picture of a Coke bottle and an arrow pointing off the highway. To the west in the distance, he spotted a cluster of buildings, the most they had seen since leaving El Alto. Maybe someone here saw Mom. At the least the stop would provide a break from driving and cold drinks and perhaps snacks, enough to keep Cap from starving. Alex exited, and Cap sat up straight.

When Alex got to the first building, he slowed. The places looked like crumbling adobe shacks, about a dozen in a semi-circle. Someone must be selling sodas as a sideline. As he passed, he scanned the porches for advertising or a soda machine. Weird how deserted this place was, like siesta time, but it was too early. Where was everyone?

Doors opened and porches that had been empty sprouted women, each holding a broom.

Cap turned. "What the…synchronized sweeping?" he said.

Alex stopped in front of the last house. He opened his door to get out.

"No!" The woman on the porch brought her broom up to her shoulder.

"That's no broom—that's a rifle." Alex slid back into his seat, slammed the truck door and grabbed Cap's arm to hold him back.

Cap slouched in his seat. "Speak really, really good Spanish to her," he said.

Alex rolled down his window and held out his empty hands. "Hola, señora. Por favor. ¿Tiene usted las bebidas frías, por favor?"

A whisper of a breeze blew at her long skirt. Dust swirled.

"Vayase. Ahora," she said.

"Got the tone," said Cap.

Just then, Veronica put her head out Alex's open window. "¡Hola!" she said.

The woman's eyes flew to Veronica and back to Alex. "Bajen. Todos. Ahora," the woman said. She motioned with her rifle.

"She says get out of the truck," Alex said.

"I'll wait here," Cap replied.

"She said everyone. Now. Do what she says. And let me do the talking,"

"Sure, sure. Got nothing to say."

"Shut up, Cap."

Cap shot him a wounded look and opened his door. From behind, Alex saw the gun handle peeking out above the strained fabric of Cap's waist-band. Alex got out, too, and put his hands up. He did not close his door, and the truck pinged an insistent reminder into the hot air as he walked a few steps away from it.

"La muchacha, también," the woman said. She kept her rifle pointed at Alex's chest.

"Verónica, ven aquí," Alex said, keeping his eyes on the woman. No movement from the truck. He turned and saw Veronica frozen like a stone statue in the truck.

"Veronica, va-moose your butto out here," Cap said. He, too, kept his eyes on the woman.

"Sí, señor," Veronica said. She hopped out over the seats, hurried to Cap and slid her hand into his. She smiled up at him.

This wasn't looking good. "Señora—," Alex began.

"Silencio," the woman said. "¿Comó estás?" she said to Veronica.

"Muy bien, señora. ¿Y usted?" Veronica replied. She bowed her head in polite acknowledgment.

"Favor de venir aquí," the woman said. She kept the gun pointed at Alex.

Veronica pulled on Cap's hand. "Okay to whatever she said," he said.

Veronica walked toward the woman. When she reached her, the woman put her arm around Veronica's shoulders.

"What's she whispering to her," Cap said.

"Shut up," Alex said through his clenched teeth.

"Hombre gordo. ¿Qué quiere usted con esta hija?" the woman said. She pointed her rifle at Cap.

"Alex, a translation would be helpful," Cap replied.

"She wants to know what the…handsome…man wants with this child," Alex said.

Cap removed his hat and bowed in her direction. "Gracias for asking, señorita boney. Coke, por favor, and—"

In a flash, she bent and squinted, hard, down the gun barrel.

"What?" Cap said. He stumbled back a step.

"Señora, lo siento. Mi amigo no habla espanol. Es muy estúpido" Alex said.

"Es verdad," Veronica said. She solemnly nodded her head in affirmation of Cap's stupidity.

"Thanks for standing up for me, Alex, but you shouldn't have called her stupid. I'm surprised rifle woman didn't shoot you for that." Cap said.

"¿Que pasa?" the woman asked Veronica.

Veronica chattered away in response, with wide hand gestures for emphasis. The woman's mouth popped open when the girl got to the part about her rescue by *los gringos valientes*. When Veronica stopped, the woman patted Veronica's back.

"Lo siento, chica. Lo siento," she said.

She lifted her eyes to the men. "Y lo siento a ustedes, señores. Y muchas gracias." She motioned for them to come up onto the porch.

Alex motioned for Cap to follow him. They climbed the wooden steps and, as directed, sat on a wooden bench pushed against the adobe wall. The woman brought out bottles of warm soft drinks and a tray of tortillas and fruit. No rifle.

Cap pointed to his chest. "Yo Cap. Y yo?" He lifted his bottle toward her.

"María Rosaria," she replied.

Alex reached into his pocket and held out the photo of his mother. "Mi madre se llama Rosaria también."

María Rosaria's hands flew to her chest. "Comó se llama usted?" she asked, her voice rising with each syllable.

"Alex...Alejandro," he replied.

María Rosaria bolted off the porch toward the other homes, waving her arms. "¡Amigas! ¡Amigas! ¡Alejandro está aquí! ¡El hijo de Rosaria está aquí!

"I think we've found your Rosaria," Cap said.

As Alex turned his head this way and that at the dizzying swirl of women surrounding them, Cap doffed his hat, repeatedly, for once, speechless. The men were led behind the homes, past a garden lush with ripening vegetables, to a long picnic table in the shade of tall pepper trees. Sit, and eat, they were instructed.

"Here's María. She speaks good English," Rosaria said. A young woman holding a squirming baby walked forward. María gazed up at Alex like he was the Third Coming.

"Your mother...," She began to weep. Startled, the baby reached its small hands upward.

"I don't think the news is going to be good here. I'm sorry." Cap said solemnly.

Alex looked away from them toward the horizon just beyond the pepper trees. He did not want to hear what was coming next. He wanted to sear these moments into his memory—the seconds before he knew. His eyes settled on red flowers blooming along thin stalks sprouting from cabbage-shaped cacti. A slight breeze waved the blossoms. From overhead, he heard a familiar "caw"; and a lone crow swooped down, then up, in the hot air. His mother's words came to him: *straighten up and fly right*. He turned back to María.

"Is my mother dead?" he asked.

"No, Alex! Your mother is fine, very fine," María replied.

Alex blew out a deep breath he didn't know he had been holding in. "Where is she?"

"Rosaria went to Flores Bonitas."

More and more Spanish flew at him, as the women interrupted each other. Alex had trouble keeping up, and the bewildered Cap hit his arm repeatedly.

"What? What?" Cap asked.

Alex held up his hand to signal, wait a minute. He didn't want to miss a word.

An hour later, Alex bent his head low as he spoke into his cell phone. "Good news! Judith, I found her. She made it to Flores Bonitas...." Fatigue and emotion caught up with him, and his voice broke.

"How is she?"

"Haven't seen her yet, but people tell me she's fine. Listen. I'm in a little place where a bunch of women live and..."

"Women? Where are you?"

Alex felt himself breathing faster. He needed her to stop questioning him, and to listen. "I'm in Bebidas Frías, a little village about 100 miles south of the border. They're married women, living together because they're related, and their men are off working in the U.S. The thing is, Mom was here for months with these women, but she's not anymore. She's gone on to Flores Bonitas, like we thought. Cap and I are headed there in a few days. Some of these women's flimsy houses are ready to collapse. We'll stick around a few days, make some repairs, repay them for taking care of Mom."

"Sure, take as long as you need. But even if you find her, she might not be well enough to travel."

Chapter 24

"Easy, you're killing me." Rosaria said. She swept a hand up toward her head, but Eliazar slapped it down.

"Don't touch. I make braids tight," Eliazar said.

In the time since she fled Shady Oaks, Rosaria had not had her hair cut. Her beauty shop permanent had dissolved into long natural waves.

"I think I'm bleeding."

"Such a baby." Eliazar yanked and twisted at the braids, and plunked multiple hairpins deep into her creation. Rosaria blinked back tears and sucked in her breath.

When she could not bear another moment, Eliazar stood back, her face reddened from her effort. "See!" she said.

Suffer to be beautiful, her mother used to say each morning as she pulled the brush through Rosaria's thick hair. Then she had been a pretty child. Now she was…her mind searched for words. The woman reflected in her mirror was…stately. Her cheeks flushed, probably from the pain of it all, and her braids formed a gray crown atop her head. She smiled at her image. Silver hoops, large enough for bracelets, dangled from her ears. *Damn, I look good!* Her hand touched the heavy cross hanging from a silver chain. *Sorry, Dear Father.*

"Here, Rosaria," Pajarito said. She nestled a silver floral barrette in the hair above Rosaria's left ear. "Single women wear flower on left side."

They dissolved into laughter.

"Don't laugh too hard, or you bust skirt," Pajarito said. "I sew long time."

"Or wet my pants," Rosaria said. The women bent over, pressing their hands into their mid-sections. "Please. Stop."

Rosaria smoothed her hand across her embroidered skirt. Red and yellow roses adorned it from top to bottom. "I love my new skirt. Thank you, Pajarito, my dear little friend."

"And what about me? Do I get no thank you?" Eliazar asked. She stood with her hands on her hips, one side out, just like the petulant girl she had been. No one had angered young Eliazar without penalty, then, or now.

"Thank you for almost killing me, Eliazar, my dear old friend."

Eliazar's youngest daughter Lola wheeled a small suitcase into Rosaria's room, and Eliazar motioned her closer. "Ah, just in time."

"In time for what?" Rosaria asked.

"You see." Lola set the suitcase on top of Rosaria's bed, unzipped it, and brought out a large plastic container. She flipped back its lid. A rainbow of cosmetics filled the interior.

"Oh, no. I don't wear makeup," Rosaria said.

Lola flicked her heavily mascaraed eyes and brilliant blue eye lids. She pursed her blood red lips. "I make you look sexy."

"I'm too old to look sexy."

Eliazar's glare said *cooperate, or else.* "Let her try. If you don't like it, you can wash it off."

Rosaria surrendered and gave herself over to Lola, who flipped a cloth around Rosaria's shoulders and went to work. Painless, at least, until she pulled hairs out of Rosaria's eyebrows, and, the ultimate insult, her chin. When Rosaria flinched, Eliazar's firm hands cupped her ears and held her in place.

"I finish," Lola said.

Rosaria held her breath. Instead of seeing the circus spectacle she expected, she saw a woman with cheeks showing the subtle flush of good health. Lips a natural gleam. Eyebrows plucked and shaped. Skin natural and glowing. *Mamá, I am beautiful again.*

"For once, she's speechless," Eliazar said.

Daniela hurried around the kitchen, arranging dishes and utensils on the table, adding two candles. "I leave now. Food in oven. You serve. And no wash off makeup."

Rosaria bristled. *How dare she tell me....* She harrumphed. Daniela had come to know her too well. To keep Daniela and all those crazy women happy, she would leave her face made up. God knows they got excited about their handiwork. You'd think they'd created the Mexican Mona Lisa.

Mario stood in the front doorway and removed his hat. *Is that bewilderment on his face?*

"Guess you're wondering why I look so—," she began.

"You are beautiful," he said. He tossed his hat onto the nearest chair.

"Thank you. The ladies helped me. They...."

His big hands drew her close. He smelled of shaving lotion, soap, with hints of hay. He nuzzled her neck and murmured something.

"What?" she said.

"You are beautiful."

She fought to form a sentence. "Yes,...you mentioned that."

"And I wish to make love to you." Mario encircled her waist with his arm and guided her down the hallway toward her bedroom.

Rosaria hid her face against his body. *Is this happening?*

Thank God for the soft rose glow of early evening, which cast her room in its best light, and her, too, she hoped. No man, other than her doctor, had seen her body since her young husband's premature death so long ago. She avoided full length mirrors, unless her body was hidden under clothing. When she did glimpse her nakedness in the bathroom, steam obscured the worst of her wrinkles. However, there was no hiding her hands, the deep brown age spots whispering to the world, *old lady*. For a woman her age, she looked good. But that was it; she was a woman her age. Before she lost her courage, she would tell him.

"Mario .... I am 73," she said.

"And I, Rosaria, am 67," he said. He led her to the bed. "Is this what you wish?"

Rosaria peered up into his flushed face. "Yes, Mario."

He stood with his back to her and began to shed his clothing. Mesmerized, she watched, until he finished and turned toward her. His torso bore the pale outline of his work shirts, his lower arms browned by long work days in the sun. On him, wrinkles added to his masculinity.

"May I?" he said, as he reached toward the top button of her blouse.

She felt a sweep of shyness, but resisted the instinctual urge to cover her chest with her hands. Instead, she nodded. She felt his hand struggle with the first button. "Shall I help?"

"Ah, my love, we have all night."

My love, he called me my love.

When he had removed the last of her clothing and dropped it to the floor, he lay beside her. She closed her eyes. She had always closed her eyes with Longino.

"Look at me," Mario said.

The hair on his chest tickled her breasts and she laughed. "It's been a long time."

He leaned over her, and she traced his face with her fingertips, then swept them across his sternum—felt a scar just below his left nipple—and brushed her fingers downward.

He was swollen already. She had done this. She had excited a man, her man.

He pulled her atop him. His body felt hot against hers. His lips kissed a breast, while his hand caressed between her legs. A sweet warmth, then a rising need, escalated into a demand that shut out everything but him, her, them.

Chapter 25

"Sorry to leave so soon, but I need to get to my mother."

"Adiós, señor, y muchas gracias," María said. Juan hung to her legs and reached for Alex. Alex ruffled the little boy's hair and backed away. The little boy's lower lip began to quiver.

"You be a good boy now." Alex hurried to his truck. "Be well, María."

"And you, señor. I...I hope we will meet again," she called to him.

After nine long days of hard labor here, he had fallen into bed each night, exhausted, but stirred by thoughts of her, how her sheer cotton blouse clung to her breasts. He imagined those breasts exposed to nurse Juan. God, she was beautiful. His next thought would be guilt; although she was a widow, he was a married man. Judith was waiting for him. Those sobering thoughts pushed him into sleep.

"I drive, señor? I very good driver," Rojo said. His hand caressed the truck's front fender.

"No thanks," Alex replied. Alex had seen the ladies' communal truck, a mass of crinkled metal with no discernible paint. No young guy with a gleam in his eye was driving his truck. He didn't even like anyone touching his truck. Even though he knew it would need a new paint job by the time this trip was over, he had to stop himself from telling Rojo to get his hands off. Rojo shrugged and hopped into the back seat.

"Cap, come on!" Alex said.

Cap backed toward the truck, bowing and dipping his hat. "Vamos con Dios!" he called to the women on the porch, who giggled behind their hands between waves.

"The señoras amour Cap," Cap said. He winked at Alex as he swung himself into the truck's cab.

As Cap reached to close his door, Veronica's hand caught it and held it open.

"Men only!" Rojo said, annoyance evident in his sharp tone.

"Por favor, Señor Cap. I go," Veronica said. Her pleading eyes locked on Cap's.

Cap turned to Alex. "Hey, man," he said.

"You know she has to stay here. They'll take care of her. She'll be safe here. After we pick up my mom, we'll stop back to see her."

"No chicas in truck," Rojo said, his voice lowered.

Cap turned his entire body toward Rojo who perched on the edge of the rear seat. "You need to be quiet, real quiet," Cap said.

Rojo slid back and slumped down, his face hidden by his baseball cap.

Cap took Veronica's small hand in his. "Veronica, no is adiós. Is…," Cap said. "Alex, how do I say, we'll be back, sweet little girl?"

Chapter 26

Rojo leaned forward from the rear seat, his hot breath on Alex's neck. "Left! Aquí! Aquí!" Rojo punched Alex's left shoulder, his method for adding emphasis to his verbal directions. As usual, his instructions came at the last minute, and in urgent Spanish and disjointed English. Rojo and Cap carried on conversations that made Alex's head ache. Alex pushed his foot down on the brake, and veered hard to the left. Dirt flew, and Alex winced at the sound of stones slamming against his truck.

"Don't these people know asphalt was invented?" Cap said. He rolled up his window against the billowing dust.

"Dirt's cheaper."

Cap reached into the bag at his feet and held out a sandwich to Alex.

"Didn't we just eat breakfast?" Alex said.

"I need to eat often, or I get faint." Cap bit deep into the bread.

"Really?"

Cap chewed and swallowed. "Yeah, really, Alex."

The miles of cacti they were driving through poked up

into the sky just like the miles of cacti they had viewed hours ago. The monotony of the miles lulled Alex into mindless driving. He yawned.

"You, okay, buddy? I can drive." Cap said.

"I good driver," Rojo said.

Alex straightened his spine and stretched back against the seat. If nothing else, the enthusiasm of Rojo for driving his truck kept him alert. No thank you.

Hours later, the endless desert landscape extended to the far horizons. Some people thought the desert beautiful; he thought it desolate. Put me out here, and I'd go crazy before long. Another pounding, this time on his right shoulder, sent them off the dirt road onto a narrower, rock-strewn, one-lane track.

"You sure about this?" Alex said. After all this time, they should be almost there.

"Sí," Rojo replied.

"How much farther?"

"A little," he said. "Little, más little."

Alex blew air out through his mouth. Mexican people would rather agree to any request—to outright lie—than to disappoint. Disagreement or answering "no" showed rudeness. Better to say "sí" and worry about truthfulness later. For all he knew, Rojo's "little more" meant they were headed in the wrong direction on a dead-end road. Meanwhile, Cap was making noises again about feeling light-headed. If they ever got somewhere, anywhere, Alex would sell his truck— maybe give it to Rojo—and he, his mom, and Cap would fly home. Enough of this.

Alex steered a circuitous path around protruding rocks and deep pot holes. His truck bounced and squeaked in protest. The sun hung low, just above the heat-seared horizon. At this rate, they might not get to town by nightfall. Alex didn't like the idea of driving in the desert's darkness out here. Suddenly, the steering wheel pulled, hard, to the right; and Alex struggled to regain control. He lifted his foot from the gas pedal, braked to a stop, and cut the engine.

"What gives?" Cap asked.

"I'll let you know," Alex answered as he swung open his door and stepped down. His boots hit the dirt road, and dust billowed up. Rojo jumped out and followed Alex around the truck.

The right front tire spilled into the dirt road like a flat puddle.

"Shit," said Rojo.

"Out, Cap. Got a flat," Alex said.

Alex scooted out from under his truck, and pulled the spare behind him. He stood and rolled the tire to the flat.

"You're the Pillsbury dust boy," Cap said. He bent and helped Alex lift the tire and push it onto the lug nuts.

"The cavalry's on the way," Cap said. He pointed to a vehicle engulfed in dust headed their way across the flat terrain. It barreled toward them, framed against the sun's dying rays.

"Not even close," Alex said. He pushed the last lug nut

into position and whirled it tight. "Get back in the truck. We need to leave. Now," he said.

Rojo pushed at Cap's back with both hands. "Hurry, señor!"

"What?" Cap said.

"Move, Cap. He's scared for a good reason," Alex said.

Before Cap's door shut, Alex started the engine and rammed the truck into gear. The wheels skidded and flung rocks as the truck bucked forward.

"How close, Rojo?" Alex asked.

"Muy, señor," Rojo said. "Rápido!" He hit the back of Alex's seat and stamped his feet as if to propel the vehicle forward by sheer force.

Alex gripped the wheel and pushed the gas pedal to the floor. Rocks leapt up and pounded the undercarriage as the truck vaulted forward. A dark SUV veered onto the road, about a half mile behind. Alex leaned forward, and willed his truck to eat up the miles.

Another blowout and they were done. He would drive on his rims before he would stop. Rocks bludgeoned the tires, and Alex winced at each blow. At this speed on this road, the tires couldn't hold up much longer. A hush descended on the cab, punctuated by the harsh whap of the tires. The SUV moved to within a few car lengths of them. A gun emerged from the passenger window of the pursuing vehicle.

Cap opened his window and raised his weapon.

"Aim for the tires, Cap," Alex said.

"Hell with that," Cap said. He fired.

The mirror image reflected the windshield exploding, and the SUV careened up over the bank of the road.

"Gracias, Jesús!" Rojo said. He pounded the interior roof with his fists.

"Easy on my truck, Rojo," Alex said.

Alex watched the cloud of dust off the road behind them…which is why he didn't see the second SUV roar up over the bank directly in front of them. He stood on his brakes, and the tires bit into the dirt. He held the wheel in a straight-ahead death grip, even though he wanted to turn the wheel, to get off the road. His truck would tip if he did. A long torturous slide, and they stopped, within yards of the SUV. It sat crosswise in the road, like a hot beast ready to attack. From the top of the darkened windows, gun barrels extended.

"Semi-automatics," Cap said.

"Santa Madre de Dios. Vamos a morir," Rojo said, his voice dropping to a whisper as he spoke.

"No one's dying today, amigo," Alex said.

"Damn right, amigo," Cap said.

Alex threw the truck into reverse, but stopped himself from pushing on the gas pedal. Too many guns, too many men, too close. They would be cut down. He took his arms off the wheel and raised them to the ceiling. Cap, still holding the pistol, brought his arms up. Alex glanced in the mirror at Rojo. Rojo slapped his hands to his face, and covered his eyes.

"Passenger with the gun, get out of the car, arms in the air," a male voice said in perfect, unaccented English.

"Alex, he's an American," Cap said. "That's good, right?" He pushed his door open and stepped down.

Chapter 27

In the late afternoon, Adriana pounded on her door. "Rosaria, Rosaria, I run all the way." She bent from the waist and gulped air.

Rosaria led her to the couch. "I ran—past tense—all the…. Never mind. What's wrong?"

"María call me. Su hijo Alejandro in her village."

"Alejandro? There? How did he end up there?"

"Say he follow your trail…from bus, to El Alto, and then to them."

An image of the bloody doctor flashed. Dios, Alex would drag her back for sure now—and to a locked facility.

"Is he still there?"

"He stay for a week. He help women fix the houses."

Why did María wait so long to call you?"

"Alejandro say he want to surprise you. After he go, she try to call, but her cell phone die."

"When did he leave?"

Adriana hesitated. "Señora Rosaria, he leave two weeks ago. American amigo with him, and he take Rojo to show them way."

Her mind swirled with possible explanations for Alex's

delay—all of them disastrous. Mexico could be a dangerous place. She wrung her hands. "They should have been here by now. I'm going to the police."

Rosaria pushed open the heavy metal door to the jail.

"La Policia is out on patrol," Caesar said. He tipped his chair back so far Rosaria waited for him to topple backwards, but years of practice had perfected his technique. He didn't have much else to do. No law breakers resided in any of his two cells today. In fact, the only time he hosted guests was on a Saturday night or a holiday, when a drunk or two threw fists and threats around, and ended up locked up for a night. Flores Bonitas was a quiet place and had, so far, escaped serious criminal activity. The police dealt with crimes no more serious than petty theft, or neighborhood disputes. And, more often than not, the residents called Father Antonio instead of La Policia. At this moment, La Policia were most than likely "patrolling" La Cantina for coffee and conchas, delicious sweet Mexican rolls.

"Gracias, Señor Caesar," she said.

"De nada," he replied.

Nothing. Sums up his job description. Around the corner, as she expected, the police car sat in front of the cantina. As she walked past the vehicle, she felt its hood. Cold. The conchas must be fresh and plentiful today. She walked into the darkened inn, and stood still until her eyes adjusted.

Comandante—as he demanded to be called—Delgado sat at a table drinking from a large ceramic mug. His left hand held half a sweet roll. From the rolls of fat cascading over his pants, he had savored many a pastry in his lifetime. His First, and only, Officer, mirrored his activity and girth across the table. Did they buy their uniforms from a costume catalogue? Epaulets of brilliant gold, with massive tassels, lined their shoulders, and the same epaulets and smaller tassels rimmed their Stetsons. Turquoise blue dominated their uniforms, with vivid red trim from shoulder to wrist on the sleeves, and around the cuff. If they ever got themselves into a shoot-out, they'd be bright targets, unless a flock of parrots flew in and provided camouflage.

"Buenos diás, Comandante," Rosaria said.

"Buenos diás, Señora Rosaria. ¿ Comó está usted?" He saluted her with his cup. The First Officer continued to eat and drink.

"Muy bien. ¿Y usted?" she replied.

Pleasantries completed, she began a condensed, and edited, version of what had occurred. Adriana brought over coffee and a roll for her, and took a seat. She punctuated Rosaria's telling with frequent interjections of, "¡Sí, es verdad!"

"And what is it you want me to do?" Delgado asked, when she had finished.

"Find him. Please," Rosaria replied.

"We are municipal police. Our jurisdiction is Flores Bonitas and the outlying area. We cannot go off searching for missing people."

"He's not missing people. He's my son. And he has an 18-year-old Mexican boy with him, plus another American."

"You need to speak to the Federales."

Rosaria walked down the steps of the cantina, across the dusty street, to the statue of Mary. Today, instead of dripping tears, broad rivulets of water streamed from the eyes of the Virgin Mother.

Chapter 28

As the vehicle roared over rough terrain, Alex, Cap, and Rojo bounced around the rear storage area and bumped against each other. Cap's soft body pushed into Alex on the right, while Rojo trembled on the left. When the men had jerked dark hoods down over their heads and tied them tight around their necks, Alex had expected gunshots. Cap and Rojo must have thought the same. Instead, the men prodded them into the vehicle, and the doors banged shut, followed by the sound of the motor starting. Sweat dripped down Alex's face, and he blinked his eyes to clear them. No air conditioning back here. Alex strained against the rope holding his hands behind his back, his efforts rewarded by burning pain as the rope cut into his wrists. Cap's quietness, atypical to say the least, notched up his fear.

"Cap?"

"Hoods? Really? Like we're terrorists?" Cap said.

Alex puffed an exhale of relief at the sound of Cap's voice. "They want to scare us."

"It's working," Cap replied. "What do they want?"

"Money. Otherwise, we'd be dead."

"How much?"

"A lot," Alex replied.

"What's the deal? They email our relatives? Alex, I've got no one who'd pay a cent for me."

Judith flashed into Alex's head—at the kitchen table, demanding credit card receipts from him for every purchase, and balancing their checking account to the penny. "Not sure I do either."

"Then what? What happens after they find out no one gives a rat's ass about us?"

Alex felt warm fluid seep onto his jeans. "You okay, Rojo?"

"Lo Siento. Piss pants." Rojo replied.

"Don't worry," Alex said.

"I think men kill us." Rojo's body shook harder.

"Us? The Three Amigos? We're getting out of this… together. All of us. Right Alex?" Cap said.

"Right, amigo," Alex replied.

A hand pushed Alex's hood up above his eyes. "See?" Cap said.

"How the…?" Alex said.

Cap nudged Rojo's hood off his eyes, too. "Old magician's trick. Turn your hands away from each other when they tie you up. Presto. Bingo. Turn your hands upright, and you're free."

"Magia," Rojo said. He grinned like the little boy he had been not so long ago.

"Cap, they have guns, lots of them. Don't do anything foolish." Alex said

"Me? Never." Cap patted Alex on his shoulder before he pushed down all their hoods.

A sudden stop, and they were there...wherever there was. Their journey had been short, no more than half an hour. Alex felt the late afternoon sun behind them, which meant they had headed east. East for half an hour. Where was that?

Alex felt hands pulling on his shirt.

"Out, Alejandro." The American voice drew out his given name—undoubtedly from his driver's license—and made it sound like a curse word. Someone poked at his back. Alex's hood fluttered away from his face in the breeze, and he saw black asphalt beneath his feet. Whoever owned this place could afford better than dirt.

Hands at Alex's elbow pushed him along and propelled him several steps. At his feet, he saw white cement. Even more expensive than asphalt. A few more steps, and he entered a building. Behind him, Cap muttered between huffs about being *a God-damn American, don't you know*, and Rojo whimpered incomprehensible Spanish. Polished wood glistened beneath Alex's dirty boots.

His fear shifted to rage. Alex didn't like not being in control—of being at the mercy of whoever these guys turned out to be. *Damn these assholes. Damn Mexico. Damn you, Mom.*

He needed to think. He knew Cap's agile mind was running through scenarios. The memory of Cap's free hands flashed into his mind. Until he met Cap, Alex had forgotten what it was like to be around someone so positive. Mom had been like that—always so energetic, involved, and enthusiastic about life. He saw, with the flashing clarity gifted to the dying, the life he'd accepted as his. If they got out of this—no, *when* they got out of this—he swore to himself, and to the

God his mother believed in that he would make changes in his life.

"Aquí, jefe. One tall American, one fat American, and a dirty Mexican kid," the American said.

"Take off their hoods, Ramon," a deep voice said in heavily accented English.

The cloth was yanked up and over Alex's head. The American, Ramon, smiled at him. His red hair and blue eyes set him apart from the three stocky Mexicans next to him. Ramon held a rifle.

Behind a massive, ornately carved desk, a big man leaned back in a chair, his hands hooked behind his head. Were those doves cut into the wood? The boss smiled, but his face stayed hard. "Welcome, gentlemen."

"What do you want from us, señor?" Alex said, as he shot a quick look at Cap. He hoped his eyes told him, *let me handle this.* Cap winked back. Alex fought the impulse to wink in return. Rojo's chin hung to his chest, like he wanted to be invisible. Alex wanted to give him a reassuring pat.

"We want nothing, but to assure your safe passage through our country."

"Thank you for your concern," Alex said.

"You are most welcome."

"Bull shit," Cap said.

Dust choked Alex. The meticulous housekeeping in the house didn't carry over to the dirt-floored enclosure. The trio stood against the rear wall, close to each other, with their shoulders almost touching. Rojo sneezed, and Alex felt spray on his arms.

"Bless you," Cap said.

"Shut up," Alex said.

"Geez, Alex."

"When will you learn how Mexico works?" Alex said.

"That a rhetorical question, or do you want me to answer it?"

"These guys value respect. You disrespect the boss, and in front of his guys, you lose. Big time."

"Yeah, I got that," Cap said.

"Why they lock us up?" Rojo asked.

"Keeping us safe, like they said," Alex replied.

"Yeah, that's right," Cap said. "They untied our hands and didn't put the hoods on again. That's good, Rojo."

Alex knew it was not good. In fact, it was bad, very bad. Showing their faces meant nothing good was going to happen. In fact, these guys wanted them to see where they were being held—in a space the size of a small car, cut into a hill, with the metal door the only way in or out. Solid dirt surrounded them, including the low ceiling. Only a foot square opening with vertical metal bars, set high in the door, permitted air to enter. When Alex thought about it too long, he got short of breath.

Alex walked to the opening and strained to see left and right. No guard posted nearby that he could see. The house sat off in the distance, separated from their prison room by an expanse of sand sprouting with low growth. In the growing dusk, he could make out two men. They leaned against the back of the house, holding their rifles as they smoked and gestured. One had red hair.

To count the days, Alex scratched small x's on the back of the door. Twelve x's so far. Their bodies smelled, and their faces itched. Cap passed the time by describing, in detail, the first meal he would eat when he got out. Rojo scratched elaborate graffiti on the dirt walls using a small stone. Alex thought only of escape. He formulated a plan, and told his companions what they needed to do. They would be ready.

On the thirteenth day, the light softened into the glow of twilight. Alex could see two figures, not the usual four, approaching from the direction of the house. This was the day. One carried a tray of dishes; Ramon, a rifle.

"Cap. Rojo. Get in position," Alex said. "Now."

Alex stood to the right of the door; Cap, to the left. Rojo squatted in view of the door, with his back pressed against the rear dirt wall.

"Get away from the door," Ramon said.

"Sure," Alex replied. He and Cap moved to the back.

"Sit down," Ramon said.

The door swung open, and the man with the tray entered. As usual, Ramon stood in the doorway watching them.

"You got gluten-free tamales there? I can only eat gluten-free," Cap said.

"You'll eat shit tamales, fat man, if I say so," Ramon said.

"Depends on whether the shit is gluten free," Cap said.

The man holding the tray bent forward to set it on the

ground in front of them. As he did, Ramon rushed in and butted the tray with his rifle, sending the dishes and food flying.

"Fat man, you eat from the dirt—like a big-mouth dog," Ramon said.

Cap launched himself at Ramon, and they tumbled into the dirt. Alex wrested the rifle away, while Cap swung punches at Ramon's gut until he folded into the ground. Rojo rode the other guy's back like a jockey, his arms tight around his captor's throat. The guy gasped for breath and whirled around, trying to dislodge the boy. Alex pulled Rojo off and pinned the guy's hands behind his back. Cap drew back a rifle and delivered a healthy tap to the back of his head. Alex caught him, mid-slump, and laid him next to his companion.

"I'll take the gun," Alex said. "Tie them up, Cap. Use your tightest, magician-proof knots."

Cap finished his task, and held up his hand. "Lookee here, amigos." He jingled a ring of keys. "Keys to the kingdom."

Alex closed the door behind them, and turned the lock. No activity from the house, as they crept toward the back. Light filtered through closed shutters in a rear room.

"More guards in the front?" Cap said.

"Likely. Let's head for the garage," Alex replied. He pointed to the left. A low wooden building stood about 50 feet away.

Cap held up the key ring. "Yeah, let's get ourselves a ride."

Cap tried the biggest key in the padlock hanging on the door, and it slipped into place. He grinned up at Alex and Rojo and bowed. A slip of his wrist, and the lock was off. Alex watched the house as Cap and Rojo swung open the double doors.

What they hadn't counted on was the automatic light that flashed on and flooded the interior with brilliant illumination. For a few moments, it blinded them.

Alex's truck sat in the front, blocking the doorway and the vehicles parked behind it. The van and a SUV stood, like impatient stallions waiting for a gallop.

Cap held up the keys and shrugged. "Can't get them out."

Alex eased the handle of his truck door, and it opened. The interior light sprang to life. He reached into the depths of his glove compartment and brought out a note-sized envelope. Alex recognized his mother's neat printing. *Extra Key.*

"One day this will come in handy, Alex," she had told him.

He had wondered at her logic. How would a key locked in his vehicle help him? Now he knew. *Bless you, Mom.* He ripped open the envelope.

"Disable the van and get in the SUV, Cap. Wait until I flash my lights. Then start up and follow me. Stay low," Alex said

"Come on, Rojo. Get in. We're getting the hell out of Dodge," Alex said.

"Dodge?" Rojo said.

Alex slipped the key into the ignition. Cap waved from behind the wheel of the SUV. Alex flicked his lights on and off, and then turned on the engine.

Chapter 29

Alex wanted to jam the gas pedal to the floor and peel out of there. Instead, he let the truck creep, its tires whispering progress. Cap tailed him, his bumper almost touching, like the second car of a quiet midnight train. With luck, they would sneak around the front of the house and be gone. Their luck held…until they rounded the corner of the house. Again, motion sensors flooded the area with light. Within seconds, shots slammed into his vehicle. Alex floored the gas pedal and slid low in the cab.

"Get down, Rojo!" Alex said.

Rojo dropped to the cab floor and rolled himself into a compact ball, covering his head with his hands.

The engine roared, and Alex's truck wheels squealed. Was Cap hit? No. Cap's headlights remained on his tail. As their vehicles lurched forward, Alex's headlights revealed a closed metal gate blocking the end of the driveway, its massive stone columns twin statements about the importance of the resident within. The gate appeared solid, too solid to risk ramming through it. High metal fences with barbed wire twisted at the top extended from each pillar. Alex slammed on his brakes, turned left, and hoped that Cap stopped before hitting him. Cap's van swerved and rocked to a stop to Alex's left. Alex opened his window.

Rojo leaped up and shouted out Alex's window in rapid-fire Spanish.

"What? What?" Cap said.

"Follow us. Rojo knows a way out," Alex said.

"You sure?"

Alex's response was to drive forward and aim his vehicle parallel to the fence. Cap pulled in behind them. Shots rang out, but they were out of range…for now.

Both vehicles bumped over the rough terrain. Rojo hung so far out the open window that Alex feared he'd tumble out. He reached across the seat and grabbed Rojo's t-shirt, and held on.

After more minutes of hurling into the night, Rojo shouted at Alex. "¡Aquí!" He pounded the exterior roof top for emphasis.

As Alex braked to a sudden stop, Rojo jumped out. Alex and Cap followed the boy's lead. The fence ended, but so did the earth—or at least that's the way it appeared.

"Lo siento, señores," he said. He pointed into the darkness. In the half moon, the hillside disappeared into bottomless blackness. "Fences for show, at front. Always end, in back. Always."

"We'll figure another way out," Alex said. He looked at Cap for affirmation. Cap continued to peer out into the canyon.

"Right, Cap?" Alex wanted Cap to come back with a smart-ass answer. "Cap?" Alex repeated.

"Hate heights," Cap said, as he stepped back from the precipice.

They decided Cap and Alex would both drive along the edge, with Rojo watching out the window for a way down. Alex knew his truck sat high above its over-size tires; plus, it had four-wheel drive. If Rojo found a passable slope, he could manage.

In the distance near the house, headlights scanned the darkness and headed toward them. Alex flashed his lights and turned them off. Cap got the message and switched his off, too.

"What're they driving?" Alex said

"Is for farm," Rojo said.

"We're being chased by a tractor?" Alex said.

"No is tractor. Is muy grande." Rojo said. He panto-mimed its girth. Is muy rápido."

Alex slowed to a stop, leaped out, and ran to Cap's vehicle.

"What's happening?' Cap said.

"We're being chased by a combine. Put the SUV in gear, jump out, and send it off the cliff."

"Got to get something out first," Cap said.

"Cap, do it. We don't have much time."

The pursuing lights bounced closer.

"Now, Cap!" Alex said.

The SUV engine clicked into drive and moved forward as Cap stumbled backward out of the vehicle. The right front wheels spun into empty air; it tipped forward, and fell out of sight. Rojo got out and let Cap climb in next to Alex.

Cap thrust a device toward Alex. Wires dangled from it. "A GPS, amigo. A genuine Mexican GPS made in China."

As Alex steered past clumps of chaparral, protruding branches screeched along his truck panels.

"¡Alto!" Rojo said.

"What do you see?" Alex asked.

"La senda. Abajo."

"What'd he say?" Cap said.

"He sees a path, down the hill." Alex said.

Alex backed up to where Rojo pointed and craned to see. *Should get out and check. No time.* With blind trust, Alex turned the truck wheels into the incline, the nose of his truck tipped down, its tail high. Alex held the wheel straight, leaned back, and pushed his foot on the brake pedal. The tires skidded over loose stones as the vehicle slid downward. Alex switched his headlights back on. He could see switchbacks in the trail, but any turn of the wheel would flip them over. He held onto the wheel, keeping it straight and true, in an illusion of control as the truck slid and fishtailed down the mountain. He smelled smoke from his brakes.

He glanced over at his companions. Rojo bounced high with every jolt. Cap's forearm extended in front of Rojo's chest, in a protective stance to keep him from sailing through the windshield. Alex gritted his teeth as the steering wheel bucked like a horse trying to throw off its three riders. A huge boulder, big as the truck, appeared at the far edge of his headlights.

Alex gentled the wheel to the left, and the passenger side of his truck scraped along the rock. The mirror tore off its bracket, and sparks flew as the rock mauled the vehicle. The good news: their encounter with the boulder slowed their descent. The bad news: from the sounds of the battle between rock and metal, Alex would need more than a new paint job.

A few more jouncing minutes, and Alex stopped the truck on level terrain. The trail had led them to a creek's edge, its waters reflecting the half moon above them. *Another blessing, Mom.* Doors flew open, and the men and boy ran to the muddy banks. Rojo waded into the creek, cupped water into his hands and slurped. Cap splashed behind him.

"We need to boil it first. He's used to it," Alex said.

Cap waddled into the water and bent forward.

"Cap, don't."

"I'm dying of thirst. How bad can it be?"

In a short time, Cap found out how bad it could be, and loudly called for death, his own.

"Hell of a weight loss program, Cap," Alex said.

"Shut…," Cap said and whirled around, heading back to the bushes.

Alex walked around his truck surveying the damage. He pulled the front fender away from the tire. All the tires seemed undamaged. The truck stood battered, but drivable. What about gas? Sweet. Their captors had filled the tank. He computed; they could get four hundred miles from here. But where was here? He began to connect the GPS.

Cap lay on the rear seat, clutching his stomach. Alex drove his truck as fast as he dared along the creek. He needed to put distance between them and the bad guys before they made camp. Plus, Cap was dehydrating fast. He required potable water, and soon.

The GPS showed them heading east, along untracked terrain, no surprise there. East was good. The creek flowed to the Baja Sur coast, north of Flores Bonitas. Seeing the name of the village on the screen made it real. According to the GPS, they were only a little over 100 miles away.

For the first time in many days, Alex felt hope. *Mom, hang on, I'm coming for you.* María and the other women had told him some nonsense about his mother being "muy bueno," but he didn't believe it. To them, an old woman who could speak a few words and get around with a cane was "very good."

Alex pulled to a stop beneath a tall multi-branched cactus. "Rojo, gather brush and built us a fire, a big one, right next to the water."

Along with the twigs for the fire, Rojo gathered other branches and roots. He dropped them into the boiling caldron, and sat stirring the mixture.

"What's cooking?" Cap asked.

"Escobilla. To drink. For mi amigo," Rojo replied.

"No thanks, good buddy," Cap said.

"He knows what he's doing. Drink it. My mom made it for me when I was a kid. Called it Butterfly Plant. Cured my diarrhea, every time," Alex said.

Rojo held out a steaming cup to Cap, and pushed it toward him.

"Oh, hell, why not?" Cap said.

Rojo grinned and ran off into the brush. When he

returned, he carried cactus leaves. Bringing a knife from his pocket, he stripped off the rough exterior and popped the remainder into his mouth. He peeled another piece and handed it to Alex. As Alex chewed, he remembered his mother's cactus salsa and how he'd loved it. Rojo's cactus wasn't as tasty, but it quieted his hunger.

Chapter 30

"Bienvenido a Flores Bonitas!" the crooked metallic sign proclaimed.

"Way to go! We're here," Cap said.

"Not quite, amigo," Alex said. He pointed ahead. A large van with "Policia" written in broad letters sat across the road. Two policemen peered from behind the hood, their guns pointed.

"Señor," Rojo said. "las policías quieren mordidas."

"Money, the police want money," Alex translated automatically.

"Whatever happened to 'the policeman is our friend'?" Cap asked. He didn't wait for an answer. "Yeah, I know, this is Mexico."

Alex braked and halted within shouting distance, half a football field of desert between them. Dust billowed from behind, up and over, and engulfed his truck. He cut the engine and pocketed his keys.

"Get out! Ahora!" Two policemen crouched behind their vehicle, their guns aimed at the trio. Even if they were lousy shots, they were close enough to get lucky.

Cap held up a fist of currency. "I speak Mexican," he said.

Alex pushed down Cap's arm and held on. "Put that away," Alex said. He increased pressure on Cap's forearm. "I talk. Only I talk."

Cap stuffed the money down the front of his shirt. "Let them find it," he said.

Alex opened his door, wide, and stepped out. He raised his hands and stood behind the door.

"Walk to the front of your truck, señor. And your passengers, out front, too." One policeman stood and waved his gun for emphasis. The other stayed low.

Cap emerged, with Rojo behind, close enough to be Cap's miniature shadow.

"What is your business in Mexico?" the officer said.

"Visiting a relative in Flores Bonitas," Alex said.

"Who is this relative?"

"Rosie…Rosaria Rodríguez."

"How are you related to Rosaria Rodríguez?"

"I'm her son. You know her?"

He swiped at his chin with his left hand. "Everyone knows Rosaria," he replied.

Alex followed the flashing lights of the police car through clouds of dirt. Even though his truck was already a mess, he flinched at the pings against his hood and hung back to escape the worst of it.

"A police escort. The policeman *is* our friend," Cap said.

Rojo hunched down, with his hat resting on his eyebrows. He had not uttered a word since their encounter with the police.

As he drove, Alex wrestled with his conflicting emotions of relief that his mother was close, and anger that she had put him through this ordeal. He felt like a father whose child runs toward the street. Does he grab the kid and embrace her, or smack the kid's behind? Right now, his emotions leaned toward the latter. And what was it about this place that brought his mother back? What did she see in this God-forsaken armpit? He saw nothing to commend it so far. Were his mother's memories of the past distorted and romanticized? Or was she delusional? She was an old woman who'd had a stroke and was on lots of medication. She wasn't capable of thinking straight. He needed to get her back to California and have her checked out by her doctor. Pronto.

After ten minutes of driving, the caravan eased into a small square. Worn wooden and adobe buildings surrounded the area. Most showed more bare wood or adobe than paint, although faded patches here and there hinted at their colorful past. In the center of the square, small bright birds swooped and sipped from a dripping statue of the Virgin Mary.

"Those birds are like ones we buy and keep in cages," Cap said, as he swiveled to keep them in his sight. "Neat that they can fly free down here."

The police vehicle slowed in front of an adobe building someone had painted red decades ago, now faded to smatterings of pink. The flashing lights of the police vehicle went off. Alex waved out his window, and the police car continued on. *La Cantina* was painted above the wooden door.

Before Alex cut the engine, Cap pushed his door open. "Just in the nick of time," Cap said.

Rojo tumbled out behind him. "¡Adriana esta aquí!" He bolted up the chipped stone steps, threw open the door, and disappeared into the dark interior.

"I guess Adriana's a good cook," Cap said.

"Don't think that's what attracted Rojo to her."

In the dim interior, a figure stood at the far end of the bar. As Alex squinted to adjust his eyes, like magic, the figure split into two.

"Mi Adriana," Rojo said.

"Estoy contento encontrarle," Alex said. He stepped forward and extended his hand.

Adriana moved tight against Rojo, who put his arm around her waist.

"You are Alejandro," Adriana said.

"Where is she?" Alex reached out to grab her arm, but Rojo's hand stopped him. "Tell me where she is."

"Señor, por favor, no touch mi Adriana," Rojo said.

The clock over the bar ticked and advanced.

Cap walked around Alex and Rojo to Adriana. "I'm Cap. Got a menu?"

The characters in the freeze-framed tableau sprang back to life. Adriana scurried behind the bar to locate a menu. Rojo sat down on a barstool, while Alex pulled out a chair at the closest table. Cap waited at attention by the bar. Adriana handed him a stained single sheet.

"You saved my life, señorita," Cap said. He swept off his hat, bowed low, and lost his balance. As he toppled forward, Alex jumped up and grabbed Cap's arm. "Easy, big fellow," Alex said.

Cap sat back. "Now this is bueno food," he said.

"Thank you, señor." Adriana continued to wipe the bar close to where Rojo sat with his head lowered over the plate in front of him. Between quick shovels of food, Rojo saluted her with his large spoon. "Sí, muy bueno, mi Adriana," he said.

Alex carried his empty plate to the bar, put it down on the gleaming surface, and stood watching Adriana as she polished and re-polished the bar.

"Thank you," he said. "Now, please tell me where I can find my mother."

Adriana kept her back to him and leaned into the bar top, scrubbing it with fierce circular motions.

Rojo placed his hand on top of Adriana's to stop her. "Adriana, Alex es un hombre bueno," Rojo said. He cocked his head toward Alex.

"He may be a good man, but is he a good son?" Adriana said.

Cap scraped his chair back. "One momento, little señorita. My amigo is muy bueno to his mom. He's Mexican, for God's sakes! Mexicans are loco for their mothers. You know that." Cap turned back to his meal, grunting into his food at the foolishness of some people.

"Por favor," Alex said.

"Please speak English to me," Adriana said. "Your mother is my teacher of English."

"Tell me what's going on here. Please." He took a step toward her. Rojo turned on his bar stool to watch him.

"First. You promise me," she said.

"Promise what?"

"Not take her back." Adriana brought the bar rag to her chest.

"But I'm her son."

"Most special because you her son."

Cap piped up from his table, "Most especially because you are her son".

"Save the English lessons," Alex said.

Cap shrugged and bent over his plate.

"I don't understand," Alex said.

"Rosaria say, 'Alejandro take me back…to the place of old people. Is horrible, horrible.'"

"No, it's not. It's a very nice place. She got good care there."

"Is a place for old people to…to die." Adriana brought a cloth handkerchief from her apron pocket and wiped at her eyes.

"She had a stroke, and couldn't take care of herself. Her own doctor told me she needed to be there."

"Rosaria tell me she hate the place."

Alex slumped onto the nearest barstool and hung his head. "She never let on she felt that way. She couldn't speak after her stroke, but…"

"She speak again, Alejandro," Adriana said. "But she say no one want to hear, so she say nada."

Chapter 31

A wild flapping of wings, followed by nothingness. Rosaria stood at her kitchen door, her hand on the knob, a large ceramic cup full of bird seed in her free hand. Something, or someone, had scared her birds. Of course, they weren't actually *her* birds, although she thought of them in that proprietary way. They were free to fly off wherever they wished, but they knew a good thing, an ample meal every morning. No need for them to forage. Instead, each day they perched in the surrounding vegetation, waiting for her to open the shutters. If she lingered too long in bed, they awakened her with chattering scolding. *Levantarse! Levantarse!* They called to her in their native Spanish.

After hesitating a moment, she went out and filled the three feeders, all within view of her kitchen table, and returned to her house to wait for her birds to return and alight in communal circles around the rims of the feeders. She wanted to eat her breakfast and, as she did, watch them dip their heads into their breakfast bowls. The smallest birds on the ground would peck up errant seeds tossed aside by the bigger ones, her morning entertainment. However, no bird show today. Who or what had scared them off?

And she was alone. She had given Daniela the day off. Mario had gone off searching for Alex, and called from a distant town to the north, reporting no evidence of him along the way. Pajarito had stayed overnight with Julio. Her son had demolished her cardboard shack—a strong push against it had done the job—and, in its place, built a sturdy one-room wooden structure. Although his new home was small and rudimentary in its amenities, Pajarito and Rosaria praised him. Each time Pajarito dropped in on Julio, she returned to tell Rosaria about the improvements he had made: he painted the exterior a bright yellow, with blue trim; he bought a bunk bed and mattresses, the lower bunk hers to use when she stayed overnight.

Rosaria moved to the kitchen window. The ocean breeze blew high through the Mexican fan palms, not reaching the lower vegetation. The ominous calm unsettled her—like the world holding its breath, waiting for what would happen next. She knew, from bitter experience, about the unpredictability of the future. Not once had she thought about her Longino dying so young. Therefore, she had not prayed for him to be well. And he had died. Her stroke struck her down with no warning. She had awakened in a hospital in a helpless state. Never saw that coming either. Anticipation was everything. God never sent the disasters she conjured. Instead, He sent unexpected ones. Therefore, Rosaria's prayers expanded daily—a thesaurus of tragedies. First, she willed her mind to think of every bad thing that could happen to her, and to everyone else she loved. Second, she asked God to spare them, one and all. Third, she prayed for the strength to survive when

God did cast upon them the calamities that—despite her best thinking—hadn't occurred to her. That about covered it.

She hadn't shared her method with Father Antonio, for she knew he would tell her it was wrong to direct God's plan. But sometimes God needed some direction. Just to be sure she didn't anger Him, she added a final disclaimer to her prayers: *Thy will be done.* And she almost meant it.

Diablo's ears stood at alert, and a low growl rumbled deep in his throat. He ran to the front door, and began to leap and bark, his sharp nails raking the floor. Rosaria peeked out the front window. Comandante Delgado pushed her gate open and approached at a rapid rate for such a big man. Rosaria held onto the window frame and closed her eyes. By the time Delgado's boots tramped up the porch stairs, she had forced herself to visualize multiple images of Alex horribly maimed, and had sent up to God frantic prayers that none of it had come to pass. Should she promise God to go back willingly, if Alex were unharmed? Before she could decide, Delgado knocked; and Diablo went crazy.

Rosaria grabbed Diablo's collar. "Está bien, Diablo," she said. He quieted.

"Your dog okay if I come in?" Delgado asked.

Best to keep the myth of Diablo's ferocity alive. "I'll come out on the porch," Rosaria said. "Diablo, stay."

Rosaria closed the door behind her, leaving Diablo to whine.

He removed his hat. "Buenas—," he began.

"Please. Tell me," she said. "Is my son alive?"

"Sí, Señora Rosaria, your son is alive and well."

Rosaria's knees felt weak.

"Where is he?"

"I brought them to the cantina. As you requested, I would not tell him where you are, and Adriana will not do so, either. He has checked into the hotel for the night."

"What happened to him?"

"He and his companions encountered some bad men. They locked them up—for money. But they all escaped. They are merely dirty and very tired."

"Who is traveling with him?"

"Rojo…. And a big American guy. I cannot remember his name in English. Sombrero, I think."

"Hat? His name is Hat?"

"And there is more. The police in Estados Unidos say you are dead, and there was a funeral…for you."

After the lawman left, Rosaria hurried to Diablo and hugged him around his thick neck. She kissed into his deep fur. "Está bien, Diablo. Está bien, Diablo," she repeated, a joyful mantra of a mother's prayers answered, followed by anguish over the pain she had caused her son. Although she knew that God read her every thought, she was glad she hadn't had time to bargain with Him—to offer her return to imprisonment for Alex's well-being. The blasphemous thought that she had outsmarted God troubled her. She feared she would be punished.

Right now, she had preparations to make. The Comandante had honored her request to keep her whereabouts secret, and Adriana would do the same until Rosaria was ready. She brought out her notebook and started a list.

The next day, Rosaria supervised a beehive of activities. Daniela cooked and sweated in the kitchen, while Rosaria laundered bedding and hung it out on lines in the sun. Pajarito even ironed the dried cotton sheets and pillowcases. In addition, she summonsed Eliazar, who arrived with daughters and a daughter-in-law to scrub, sweep, and dust throughout Rosaria's home.

Julio delivered a banister he had carved for her and hammered it into place along the edges of her porch. She had asked him to fashion one with a few roses here and there. Instead, rose buds topped every railing, with long curved stems extending to each base. In addition, he directed hired workers who trimmed the bouganvillea and set new flowering plants in barren garden spots. Afterward, they raked the yard and swept the walkway. Before Julio left, he brought her to her front door. He stretched up and took down her Crazy Lady placard. From behind a chair, he brought out another sign. This one was as long as the horizontal door frame. Fully open rose blossoms framed the words Julio had carved: *La Casa Feliz de La Señora Rosaria*. She smiled up at it. Yes, this was a happy home…and it was hers.

After everyone left for the day, Rosaria and Pajarito walked from room to room. Hints of bleach and furniture polish wafted throughout the interior. With the windows open, by morning the air would be fresh again. Daniela had been sent home early, and Rosaria carried the plates of tortillas and carne asada to the front porch. She and Pajarito settled in chairs to eat. Pajarito picked at her food.

"Are you feeling well? You worked too hard today," Rosaria said.

"I'm not such an old woman that I can't do a day's work," Pajarito said.

"Of course you're not. I just thought that maybe you overdid."

"Well I didn't." Pajarito's lower lip pushed out, and Rosaria recognized the childhood pout.

"Pajarito, what's wrong?"

"Your son is coming. He will take you away from here."

"I'm not going anywhere."

"But…"

"Remember when we were little girls and swore promises to each other? We always kept our word. When my parents took me to America, we swore we would never forget each other. And we didn't. I swear to you now, dear Pajarito, I will never leave you. We will become old ladies together…oh, we've done that already."

Pajarito's protruding lower lip dissolved into an upward curling of her lips.

"Is that a smile I see on that beautiful face?"

"You always make me laugh, Rosita."

"And I always will." Rosaria reached for Pajarito's hand.

"What will you say to Alex?"

"I will say, 'Welcome to my home, son.'"

Chapter 32

"You want to go shopping?"

"All we got is what we're wearing. Not exactly going-to-dinner-at-mom's clothes." Cap patted the front of his shirt, and dust flew. He pointed to Alex's stained and torn jeans.

"Didn't see any mall driving in here."

"No mall required. Adriana will direct us to the local men's store. No problema." Cap tipped his invisible hat to Alex and retreated into the hallway. "No problema," he repeated as he closed the door behind him.

Alex sat on the bed and held his forehead in two hands. He ran his fingers through his long hair. He held up his right arm, bent his head toward his arm pit, and sniffed.

Adriana smiled when Cap inquired about the nearest men's clothing store, and now Alex knew why. The nearest men's store was close; in fact, it came to them in the cantina. An ancient gnome of a woman hobbled to the table where Alex, Cap, and Rojo were eating. A worn tape measure hung around her neck. She motioned for them to stand, and whipped her tape around them in every direction. When she pantomimed spreading their legs, Cap didn't move. She pushed at his legs.

"Be careful down there, señora," Cap said.

After more measurements, that she scribbled on a fragment of paper, the old woman mumbled to Adriana and left.

"What did she say?" Alex said.

"She will bring your clothes here tomorrow at noon."

"Don't mean to be rude, señorita, but is that noon, Mexican time?" Cap said.

"You are learning our customs, señor. You will have your clothes in time for your evening with Rosaria."

As the men walked along the colonnade, vendors' stands appeared in the distance.

"Let's go buy ourselves some new hats," Cap said. He picked up his pace.

Cap settled on a huge sombrero the size of a small umbrella.

"Cap, you look like a Mexican cartoon character," Alex said.

"Just the look I'm aiming for," Cap said.

Alex and Rojo chose more subdued head gear: blue baseball caps with a bull embroidered in gold thread on each.

Cap commanded they all buy sandals. Alex objected, until he tried a pair on and felt their unconfining comfort, a marked improvement over irritating boots and rumpled socks. Rojo tore off his old rubber flip flops, tossed them away, and slipped into his new leather sandals.

"Serapes!" Cap said. He led the way to the next stand. The sales girl pulled an extra large serape from the bottom of pile and flipped it up and over his shoulders.

"Es muy hermoso, señor," she said.

"What do you think, guys?" Cap asked.

'It's you, Cap," Alex said.

"Sí, is you." Rojo said.

"Damn, amigos, this has been quite a trip," Cap said. "Wouldn't have missed it."

"Me, también," Rojo said. He placed his cap over his heart.

"There's a photographer. We need a photo of the tres amigos." Cap pushed them toward an elderly man with an equally ancient camera. "¡Señor, por favor!"

Alex posed with the men, his face a stern rebuke to the wide smiles of the other two. These guys could afford to fool around. He couldn't. His mom needed him, and they just didn't get it.

"You should buy something for your mom," Cap said. "I'll help you find something."

As they walked, Cap perused each stand, most filled with hand-painted Mexican pottery, until he held up a silver pin in the shape of a rose bud. "It even has some thorns. Perfect for her," Cap said as he handed it to Alex.

Around two in the afternoon, the sellers covered their wares with cloths and tarps, and hurried away in a group. Each carried a chair or a blanket.

"Siesta time?" Cap asked one.

"No, vamos a la casa de la Señora Rosaria," he called back over his shoulder.

"What did he say?" Cap asked.

"He said they're going to Rosaria's house," Alex said.

"To your mom's house? Why? What's happened?"

"Nothing good." Alex picked up his pace and followed the crowd down a path away from the beach. Rojo kept up.

"Wait up," Cap struggled to flip his sandaled feet faster.

Alex broke through the path into the open, with Rojo on his heels and Cap huffing further back. People streamed through a gate and onto the porch of a house. Unbidden, memories surfaced and flooded over him. His mother had brought him here, to this very place, the summer after his father died, to the house of her parents. And for several summers more, he remembered the tedious bus ride, no air conditioning then, squirming next to the window and watching for the first sight of the sea. After his grandparents' deaths, their trips had ceased. No one was here for her anymore, his mother said. Why, then, had she fled here? Was she trying to regain her childhood?

The adobe exterior, the long front porch, the bougainvillea climbing the wall—all looked the same—but brighter. Today's throng placed their chairs on the porch until it was full, and the overflow positioned their chairs and blankets in the yard facing the porch. What was going on?

The crowd buzzed with loud chatter. When the front door opened, the men, as one, removed their hats. A regal woman emerged, and the buzz quieted a bit. *Mom?* Her braided gray hair was wound atop her head. A yellow serape embellished with big red flowers covered her shoulders, and a flowing red skirt hung to her sandaled feet. From the house, a huge dog trotted to her, its massive head reaching above her waist. The people seated closest to them slid their chairs back. His mother settled into a high chair near the door, raised a book in her hands, and the crowd hushed. The dog sat next to her, his serious face surveying the crowd.

"Buenas tardes, amigas y amigos," Rosaria said. "Today I will speak English. Do not worry. I will read to you in Spanish." Her words rang out, clear and precise.

The crowd applauded. "Good! You speak English ahora," someone called out.

"We understand mucho, señora," another said.

"You good teacher."

"Thank you," Rosaria said. "Last time I read, I stopped on page 57. Who remembers what was happening in the story?"

A middle-aged lady stood up from her chair in the yard. "Señora say 'Go' to hombre."

"That's right. The lady said, 'Go away' to her lover." Roaria replied. "Who knows his name?"

"Pepe!" several voices called in unison.

"Good! The man's name is Pepe. Repeat this sentence after me: 'The man's name is Pepe.'"

A wave of voices echoed the sentence, ending in a crescendo.

"And the lady's name is Helena."

Again, a swelling echo.

"Good for you," Rosaria said. She raised her hands and clapped for them. Return applause enveloped the crowd.

Rosaria waited until they quieted, raised her book, and began to read in Spanish. Her Spanish floated like song lyrics over the yard, reaching the three men beyond her gate.

The reading over, people dispersed. Some hung back to have a word with Rosaria. They formed a line leading up to the porch where she sat.

"Your mom's a celebrity here," Cap said. He had removed his sombrero when Rosaria began to read and still held it in his hands.

"Is good book," Rojo said.

"Let's get out of here," Alex said.

"We need to talk about this." Cap gestured toward the lone chair in Alex's room. "Why are you upset?"

"Upset? Upset?" Alex strode over to the chair, picked it up with one hand, and tossed it against the far wall.

Cap retrieved the chair, and held it aloft. Its legs wobbled. "Feel better now that you've killed it?"

"Shut up."

"Nope. Never shut up, never give up. Not the Caporali way." He turned in his best big man pirouette and bowed forward over his belly.

"You're a piece of work."

"Why thank you, Alejandro, mi amigo, mi capitan." Cap winked.

Despite his best effort, Alex's scowl morphed into a smile.

"That's better," Cap said.

"Nothing's better."

"Sure it is. We got here in one piece. You're pissed because your mom made some choices…better than yours maybe. She talks fine and looks great, all tan. And she moves like a young woman. Not at all what I expected."

"Not what I expected either. Don't be fooled by seeing her for a few minutes. I'm going to do whatever it takes to get her out of here and take her home."

Chapter 33

Before the guests could push open the garden gate, Diablo leapt at the front door and bellowed his early warning.

"My nerves can't stand this," Pajarito said. She put a trembling hand on Rosaria's arm. "What if he takes you away tonight?"

"Pajarito, I promise. You and I will be here on the front porch after they leave—talking about the wonderful visit from my handsome son."

Pajarito gripped her arm. "I am not so sure as you."

"Go into the living room." Rosaria tapped Pajarito's arm. "And breathe."

Voices approached, and steps sounded on her porch. She stood back from her door and waited for someone to knock. For several moments, she allowed Diablo to bark and jump at the door before she drew him back and clicked the leash onto his collar.

"Good boy. Alex is here." She held his leash tightly and opened the door. Alex stood next to Cap. El Comandante, Adriana, and Rojo crowded the porch behind them.

"Mom," Alex said. He pushed past El Commandante and wrapped her in a long, fierce hug.

Rosaria leaned her face again his chest and returned his embrace. "I'm so glad you're safe," Rosaria said. She looked up at him.

His eyes glistened, and he swiped a hand across them.

"Welcome to my home, son," she said.

"Now that's a dog," Cap said. Both his hands held a massive sombrero in front of his body like a shield. "I'm Cap. Wow…you look terrific, Mrs. Rodríquez."

"Call me Rosaria, please."

Like a protective doorman, Diablo's nose checked out each person as they filed past. When the hefty lawman sidled past, he watched Diablo for any aggressive movement.

Rojo and Adriana held hands as they entered. Rojo removed his cap and bowed his head. "Señora Rosaria, eres hermosa," he said.

"Sí, Rosaria, you look like una reina…a queen," Adriana said. She released Rojo's hand and bent down to Diablo. "Bueno Diablo," she said. Diablo took a meat morsel from her extended hand.

"There's a dog I can relate to. He likes women and food," Cap said.

"Sí, sí, señor," the sheriff said. Now that he was safely past Diablo, his posture relaxed. He turned back toward Rosaria. "Ah, señora, if I was a single man…"

Adriana and Rojo sat tight against each other on the appropriately named love seat. Private exchanges in Spanish set them apart from the others. Rojo had a lot to tell her.

Pajarito, struck mute by the assembled group and all their English, sat back in her chair, like a small child wishing she could escape to her room. Rosaria reached over to pat her hand. Pajarito sent a small smile her way.

"Mrs....Rosaria, I would not have recognized you from the photo Alex showed me," Cap said.

"Yes, I have changed a little," Rosaria said.

"And we were so impressed with your reading to the crowd yesterday," Cap said.

"You were here?" Rosaria said.

"She reads to us every Monday and Wednesday afternoon, exactly at three," Adriana said. "They give up their siestas to hear her read. And they show up on time. When it is three, she begins."

Daniela carried in a tray of food, and beckoned them to follow her. "Favor de comer," she said.

"I understood that, beautiful señorita," Cap said.

Daniela's cheeks colored the shade of ripe tomatoes, and she pivoted toward the dining alcove.

Alex extended his hand to help Rosaria up. She stood up without assistance, smiled up at him, and placed her hand on his arm. "Come see what a good cook Daniela is," she said. "She has made all your favorites."

Mexican pottery, piled high with traditional foods, lined the center of the table. Brightly painted floral plates with folded white, rose blossom embroidered napkins sat at each place setting.

"What a spread," Cap said. His eyes shone like he had just come upon his own personal Holy Grail.

After everyone was seated, Rosaria tapped her glass with her fork. "Please, let us pray," she said.

Cap put down the serving spoon for the rice, and bowed his head.

"Thank you, dear God, for bringing Alex, Rojo, and Cap safely to my home. Bless us all with continued good health and harmony. Thank you for the bountiful food you have provided for us. In your name, we pray. Amen."

"Amen" rang around the table, followed by the clang of utensils.

Rosaria and Alex rocked in adjoining chairs on the front porch. Adriana and Rojo drifted past them down the steps for a walk, taking Diablo with them. El Comandante and Cap helped Daniela carry dishes into the kitchen, and had not emerged—undoubtedly remaining there to eat the scraps left in each serving dish and lick the big serving spoons.

Alex held out the rose pin. "This is for you, Mom."

"It's beautiful, Alex. Thank you." She attached the jewelry to her white blouse and reached for his hand, brought it up to her lips, and brushed it with a kiss—just as she had done when he was a small boy and had skinned his bare knees on the asphalt. "I'm sorry I caused you so much worry and trouble."

Alex stopped rocking and turned to her. "How could you leave without a word to me? The police said you'd drowned in the ditch behind your house. Mom, I had a... a memorial service for you."

The calls of the jungle birds filled the evening.

"If I had told you my plans, you would have stopped me."

"Darn right I would have. Mom, the place here is nice, and you seem to be feeling better. But…it's only temporary. What happens when you're not fine? You need to see a doctor, get your medications refilled."

"I have seen a doctor, my doctor, Dr. Ruiz."

"Where'd he get his diploma—Tijuana Tech?"

"Alejandro. His diploma has Johns Hopkins printed on it."

"Johns Hopkins? Then what's he doing here?"

"He was born here. He remembers what it was like with no doctor."

Alex shrugged. "Mom, you can't stay here. These people and a dog; they're not your family. Judith and I are your family."

"Alejandro, you must listen to me. I had become an invisible old woman—even to you—sitting in God's waiting room, waiting to die. No one saw me; no one heard me. Here I have discovered my life again. I have people who count on me, who value me. Alejandro, I have people who *see* me."

Cap pushed out the front door. "Oh, there you two are. I think I'm in love."

Chapter 34

Rosaria could not quiet her thoughts and fall asleep. When she closed her eyes, Alejandro, the little boy, grasped her hand at his father's funeral—too young to understand why the adults were crying, and frightened by his mother's grief. Aferward, they cried together, but her sorrow outlasted that of her little boy; and she learned to save her tears for late at night to spare him.

But she hadn't spared him this time, and hadn't even tried. She had run away—no explanation left behind—desparate to escape and angry at him. Justified. Meanwhile, she made friends and found Mario, while her son mourned her death. Even worse, he had endangered his life coming for her. And tonight, Alex, the grown man, had sat on her porch, unwilling to see that she belonged here.

"Mom, why are you choosing this life?" he had asked as he left.

"You said it, Alejandro—I'm choosing *life*."

The clock in the living room chimed eleven times. She forced herself to breathe in and out; count each intake and outtake of breath, synchronized to the ticking clock. Tears trickled down her cheeks and onto her pillow.

Diablo cocked his head as if he were trying to translate her language into his.

"I'm, fine, good boy Diablo," she said. "Just sad."

As Rosaria stroked his big head, he exhaled and nestled deeper into the palm of her other hand. His whiskered snout tickled. Rosaria laughed out loud at her splendid companion. Until Diablo, she had never understood why people got so crazy over their pets. Not that she would ever diminish Diablo's place in her life by calling him a pet. He was family. How dare Alejandro say she was alone?

Diablo raised his head and grumbled a throaty growl that crescendoed to loud barks. As he padded to investigate, knocks sounded on the front door. Rosaria rolled out of bed. Diablo barked and sniffed with his long snout into the cracks along the door frame. Satisfied that he recognized a friend, he allowed Rosaria to nudge him aside. She trusted Diablo's instincts, but said a cautionary "Who is it?"

"Mario. Sorry to arrive so late," he said.

She opened wide. "Mario." She fell against his chest and pulled herself tight against him.

"Didn't know you were so strong, little one."

"I'm so relieved you're back."

"Me, also."

"Thank you, for trying to find my Alejandro for me." Rosaria leaned into him and hugged him around his waist.

"He is here. Now you can stop worrying."

"Yes, you are right. Time for me to stop worrying. Come, soak in my tub, and I'll wash your back."

Mario scooped her up in his arms and closed the door

behind him with his foot. He carried her like she weighed nothing. "Hola, Diablo."

At the bedroom door, the dog sat.

Mario laughed. "He knows the routine, doesn't he?"

Rosaria bent over Diablo. "You're still my number one guy," she said. She winked up at Mario. Diablo settled into his dog bed and curled his body. He closed his eyes.

"Oh, Mario, Alex wants to take me back to…that place. He pretended to listen to me, but I know him. He hasn't changed. He's the same son who put me into that awful place. Assisted living. Should call it assisted *dying*."

"What exactly did he say to you tonight?"

"He says I can't live alone down here, questions Dr. Ruiz's qualifications. Mario, I can't forget what he did—sold my house without telling me." Her eyes welled with tears.

Mario encircled her in his arms. "He loves you, Rosaria."

"I love him, too. But he…he sold my *home*," she said. She breathed to the clock ticking away the seconds. "I can't trust him. He wants to 'yes, but' me until I'm back in that prison again waiting to die."

"That will not happen. I will not permit it to happen."

She had a home, a man, many friends, a dog. Her son was safe.

"Gracias, Dios," she whispered into the darkness.

Mario got up early and took Diablo out.

Time to wash my face, and, yes, apply a hint of foundation. Rosaria splashed her face with water. Eliazar's daughter had created a makeup monster. Ever since her friends' intervention, Rosaria didn't feel completely dressed until she had applied her new face, the attractive one that makeup brought out. She didn't think of it as covering up. No, she was coming out—to show her previously hidden beauty—and she laughed at her new-found vanity. She smoothed foundation across her face, and a light splash of color onto her cheeks and lips. Better.

She chuckled at the memory of Mario's face the first time he saw her after her make-over. Speechless. No words were necessary. His actions told her everything.

Today he kissed Rosaria good morning, and left. He had been gone too long in his futile search for Alejandro. His ranch needed his supervision.

When Rosaria waltzed into the kitchen for breakfast, Pajarito and Daniela stood close and whispered at the sink. Without hearing their words, she knew what was going on. They were worried that Alejandro would take her back to Estados Unidos by force. That's how things happened down here. Her reassurances hadn't convinced them otherwise.

Rosaria attempted cheerful conversation, but gave up. Daniela retreated to the sink to wash and bang her metal pots. By the noise, no pot was spared.

Pajarito excused herself and went to her bedroom. "I am very tired today," she said.

Rocking and petting Diablo lulled Rosaria into a contemplative place. Although every morning and evening she talked to

God in her prayers, this morning Mario's whispered words, after their lovemaking, blocked her brain from any godly thoughts.

"Marry me, Rosaria."

She rocked too fast, like she was trying to propel herself into the future and see it. Now. Diablo pushed at her hand, to remind her that he was here, that he expected his head to be petted. She slowed her rocking, and attended to him.

She had so many questions. Did Mario really mean it? Or was he asking her, just to rescue her?

"What shall I do, Diablo?"

His face, a blank of contentment, offered her no answer.

As she rocked, her mind calmed, and intuitive thoughts surfaced. If not those of a deity, they felt true and right.

Chapter 35

Alex rolled over in bed and grabbed his watch from the nightstand. God, his head pounded and his throat hurt. Sweat plastered his clothing to his body. Why hadn't he taken off his clothing? He remembered drinking, a lot, and arguing with Cap. He reached for the pitcher and chugged water from it. He pushed himself upright, and his head protested. Time to head down the hall for a shower.

Alex felt Adriana watching him from behind the bar. His head felt like a heavy, aching mass, and he bent over a table, his hands pressed against his face shielding his eyes. It had been a long time since he'd felt so hung over. He couldn't hide his misery, even though he knew she'd run and tell his mom. What he did was his business, no one else's. He didn't need his mother telling him what to do. He raised his head and forced himself to sit up straight. He pushed the rice, beans, and egg mixture around his plate with a tortilla.

"Is the food good?" Adriana asked.

"Yeah. Not hungry," Alex replied. He stared out the

window at the dusty town square. Two small dogs growled and tussled in the dirt. They rolled over and over in mock battle, until they tired of their game, shook themselves off, and trotted out of sight.

Adriana refilled his coffee cup, and sat down across from him with her own cup. "How much longer will you be here… to visit your mother?" Her hands cradled her coffee, and she kept her eyes on the cup. "I worry—many of us worry—that you will take Rosaria away from her home here with us."

"She has a home with me."

"So…you want her to live with you?"

Unswallowed food caught in his throat. He choked and grabbed for the coffee. "Sorry, went down the wrong way."

Adriana leaned forward. "You want her to live with you," she said, this time as a statement.

Alex smeared his face with a napkin. "You don't understand. My mother needs to live in a facility…a place with people there who can take care of her."

"You, her son, can take care of her, in your home."

"I have my own business. I work long hours. My wife… she didn't sign up to be a nurse." He repeated the words Judith had hurled at him right after Rosaria's stroke.

Adriana turned away and pushed through the swinging doors into the kitchen. Both sides slammed into the adjacent walls.

"Who does someone have to kiss around here to get breakfast?" Cap stepped into the room. "Coffee, pors favors, sweet señorita," he called in the direction of the kitchen. "Too much tequila for us last night, right amigo?"

Alex nodded his head in slow agreement. "Have a seat. And keep your voice down."

"Sorry. My head feels like I bounced it off a brick wall. How about yours?" Cap asked.

Alex waved his hand in a dismissive gesture. "I'll live."

"Living's good. So, what's our plan for today?"

"Thought I'd take a walk over to see Mom."

"Oh?" He raised his chin. "I'll go along with you."

"That necessary?"

"While you see your your mom, I'll spend time with Daniela, a looker and a cooker, dynamite combo."

Adriana set a full plate in front of Cap, and he pulled it closer. "I'm talking about you, too, Señorita Adriana."

The hot day grew hotter as they trekked to Rosaria's house. The fetid jungle smells conjured boyhood memories of trips to his grandparents. He had reveled in running and leaping through the high growth, until the ground turned to sand, and the sand to water; and he had sped at full speed into the surf. He dived into the water, scattering the startled fish, and shot to the surface. When it came time to return to California, he cried along with his mother and her parents. He wanted to stay in this boy's heaven on earth…forever. He hadn't understood his mother's explanation of poor conditions, no work for her.

Alex knew better than to think Cap's only motive in coming along was to see Daniela. Cap would be listening and watching. Let's hope Daniela had something delicious on the stove or in the oven, and Cap's nose would lead him directly to the kitchen, and keep him there.

"Like walking in a steam room. Must have lost ten pounds already." Cap removed his ever-present sombrero, wiped his face on his shirt sleeve, and fanned himself with the straw hat.

"Yeah, I'd forgotten how hot and humid it gets here. Never bothered me when I was a kid. I'd just run like mad and jump into the ocean."

"Don't know about running, but jumping in sounds good. I can hear the surf. How about we do that now—cool ourselves off?"

"No swim suits."

"No problema."

Alex spun around.

"Alex…. I meant we can buy suits from a stand down there. I know better than to shock the locals."

Alex hesitated. He could smell himself. Between him and Cap, his mother might faint from their odor. A dip in the ocean would cool them off and clean them up.

The breeze off the ocean tempered the heat. Alex breathed in the fresh air. Gentle inflow of sea water headed toward the shore. Sea birds called. This place smelled and sounded familiar.

"Alex, come on! Got to dip your toes into the Sea of Cortez," Cap said over his shoulder as he stood a few feet into the water.

At the sight of Cap posing like a muscle magazine cover model, Alex shook his head. Cap's new muy-muy grande, orange and yellow striped bathing suit stretched tight across his body. Garish as hell, but Cap didn't seem to mind. Plus, it had been the only one large enough for the big guy. By comparison, Alex's brown bathing suit paled. His robin to Cap's peacock.

"I see you covet my swimming attire...and my body," Cap said.

Alex lunged at him. Cap dodged and pushed Alex out into the surf. Alex fell to his knees in the sandy bottom, righted himself, and rolled over to float. Cap threw himself backward and floated in the water, like a benign, multi-colored whale.

The warm salt water cradled Alex in buoyant contentment, and the gentle waves rocked him. He relaxed and closed his eyes to the sun high in the sky. Worries about his mother, about his wife, about his business drifted off. He was here, in this moment, and it was good, all good. Wish the rest of my life could be like this...unrealistic, but still.... His mind took him to his mother; she beamed radiance... and happiness. How long since he had seen her like that? He stretched and yielded to the sea's relentless motion.

"What're you smiling about?" Cap asked.

"Thinking back to being here as a kid. We really liked to..." Alex drew out "really" into two long syllables. At the same time, he reached over and grabbed the back of Cap's trunks. As he pulled down, he leaped on top of Cap and pushed him under.

Cap sputtered and spit out water as he surfaced. "Oh, yeah?"

Alex paddled furiously out from shore, but, before he could escape, Cap dove on top of him. Alex felt his body submerge under Cap's full weight. He struggled to the surface, and lunged at his combatant. Too tired to keep up their water battles, they resorted to spitting water at each other. Finally exhausted, Alex and Cap stumbled ashore and stretched out on the wet sand.

Cap raised his head and spit a final mouthful of water onto Alex's chest. "Trying to drown me?"

Alex lay back on the warm sand and closed his eyes. He woke himself with his own snoring. Cap sprawled three feet away, his hands behind his head. He rolled toward Alex. "This is living."

"For a vacation. Who could live here?"

"I could—slow pace, great food, knock-out gorgeous señoritas. What more could a guy want?"

"A way to earn a living. And my mom isn't safe in this place. That crap border doctor might trace her here; we did. And some of these local characters look dangerous."

Cap shook his head. "When they look up 'stupid shit' in the dictionary, your picture must be there. What you don't know is your mom is good friends with the most powerful man here—and maybe for hundreds of miles around. He's not going to allow anyone to mess with Rosaria."

"Who's this guy? You telling me my mom's friends with a drug lord?"

"He's no drug lord, but everyone knows better than to

cross him. You have no idea what's going on here. He's the reason you and I are enjoying our day at the beach, and not buried in a shallow grave out in the desert. And the only thing saving you now is that you're Rosaria's son."

"What're you talking about?"

"El Commandante told me last night. According to him, those thugs were tracking us. He said they're relentless, they wouldn't have stopped until they found us—but no one, not those guys chasing after us or that dumb doctor chasing after her, dared follow us into this town. Rosaria's friend with this guy Mario, and he's the man down here."

"I didn't meet any Mario at her house."

"That's because he was off searching for you."

"How do you know all this?"

"I'm a private detective. I detected: asked questions, listened to the answers. This Mario guy won't permit anyone to come into this town to get us, and he sure won't let anyone harm your mother."

"What's this so-called important guy want with my mom?"

Alex's wet suit clung to him, and the sand against his skin chaffed. As he walked on the path through the vegetation, he began to dry and the sand fell away. When Cap attempted conversation, Alex didn't reply. *Good friends?* What, exactly, did that mean? How did his mother become friendly with a Mexican tough guy? Further proof to him that she wasn't in her right mind. And Cap staying here? That had to be just talk, or had he lost his mind, too?

Behind him, Cap plodded and huffed. "You're killing me. I'm dying. Right here. Right now. Bury me under that palm, over there."

Alex halted. "Almost there. There's Mom's house, just past those high bushes. See the tile roof?"

"Praise the Lord. I think I can make it that far." Cap set off, leading the way, the plow horse with the stable in sight. "Hope Daniela knows mouth-to-mouth resuscitation." he said over his shoulder.

Cap stopped suddenly, and Alex almost ran into him. "What?" Alex asked.

"That must be Mario—the man I told you about. There, on the porch with your mom."

A big man stooped over his mother, his arms around her, his lips on hers. Alex pushed past Cap.

Chapter 36

Alex focused on the man striding down the porch steps and across the enclosed yard. Like he owned the place. This guy was tall and muscled, the physique of someone who did manual labor. He looked like one of her workmen dressed in his Sunday best. Pearl snaps adorned his heavy shirt, which was tucked into his jeans. With his hand on the gate, the man turned to wave to Rosaria. She touched her heart and blew him a kiss. *Good God.* As soon as he turned and stepped through the gate, Alex was there.

Mario extended his hand. "I'm Mario. You must be Alejandro," he said in slightly accented perfect English. "Your beautiful mother was so worried about you. She asked me…"

"I know who you are. You stay away from my mother!" Alex threw a wild punch—intended for the jaw, but hit him mid-chest, instead.

"¿Qué demonios?" The man stumbled backward.

Alex leaped at him, his fist drawn back to deliver another blow. Cap grabbed him from behind and held onto him. "Stop it! Alex! Stop it!"

"Let go of me." Alex wrenched out of Cap's grip and lunged forward.

Without the element of surprise, Alex was no match for his opponent. Some brief, futile pummeling, and Alex found himself face down on the ground, his arms pinned behind him. Pebbles bit into his sweaty face, and his soggy bathing suit pasted itself against his body. "Let me up!"

"Alejandro! What is the matter with you?" His mother's look was the angry one she had saved for those occasions when, as a boy, he had really screwed up.

"Take your hands off me."

"No. Don't let him up...until he promises to behave himself."

Cap bent down. "Listen to your mom."

"Yes, I agree. Listen to your mother," Mario said. Alex felt himself being lifted to his feet.

"Mario, I am so sorry. Are you hurt?" Rosaria touched Mario's arm. "And you!" She whirled around. "Alex, I can't believe you. You need to apologize."

Alex spit dirt from his mouth. "Who the hell is this guy?"

"Mario is my special friend."

"If he's so special, how come you never mentioned him to me?"

Mario stepped forward.

Cap put out a restraining hand on Mario's arm. "Easy, man," Cap said. "He's not thinking straight. Where his mom's concerned, he's muy loco."

Alex clenched his fists. He wanted to punch somebody.

Rosaria took Mario's arm, and gestured toward the porch. "Come, Mario, sit down and catch your breath." She led Mario back toward the house. "Alejandro, you come, too," she said over her shoulder. "And clean off that filth before you come up on my clean porch."

Alex hesitated, then followed, with Cap so close he could feel his hot breath on his neck.

"Back off," Alex said.

Alex stopped at the bottom step and brushed off his shirt and shorts.

Rosaria gestured to an empty chair. "Sit down, Alejandro." Mario stood behind her, his hand on the chair back. "Cap, come up here with us."

"I'll go around to the kitchen door and check on Daniela. Yell if you need me." Cap disappeared around the corner of the house.

Alex kept his eyes on his mother.

"Mario and I met soon after I arrived. He and I have become close…"

"How close?"

"You are being rude. Mario left his ranch and was out for days searching for you. I was going crazy thinking the worst had happened to you. He insisted on going out looking for you himself."

"Still doesn't explain why you didn't at least mention him when I was over here."

"It wasn't the right time."

"Is there ever a right time to hear your mother tell you she's making a fool of herself."

"You will not speak to your mother in that manner," Mario said.

Rosaria reached toward him. "Mario…"

"I see only one fool sitting on this porch." Cap stood in the doorway holding a tray of glasses, with Daniela behind him. "Hey, anyone ready for lemonade?"

When the men and Rosaria sat with a drink in one hand and a pastry in the other, Cap nodded his head toward them. "Our work here it done. Vamos, Daniela!" He bowed and held the front door for Daniel to enter.

"Delicious…as always," Mario said.

"Yes, Daniela spoils us with her desserts, doesn't she?"

Alex took note of the plural "us."

"If I don't watch myself, I'll get fat." Rosaria giggled.

"So, Mom, after Mario goes on his way, how about you and I take a walk? It's really nice down by the beach." He settled back into his seat. Alex raised his cup and sipped. *I'll outwait the bastard.*

The men made their way back to their hotel rooms through the cooling early evening. Alex didn't feel like talking, but, as usual, Cap did. "Did you and your mom come to an understanding?"

"Couldn't really talk to her. That guy wouldn't leave."

"I got to tell you something I never told you. When you first hired me, I went over to Shady Oaks. That place was damn depressing—old people, half asleep, parked in wheel-chairs in the halls. Others alone in their rooms, eyes glued to TV's. An hour before meal time, they all shuffled down the halls to the lobby, and sat at the dining room door, waiting for the only excitement in their day—the next meal."

"You're exaggerating. It wasn't that bad. I went there almost every day. You were there only once."

"You saw what you wanted to see. What I saw made me not so sure I wanted to find her and bring her back. Let her alone. She's found someone. She's happy. Case closed, as far as I'm concerned."

"I'm not going home without her."

"Alex, I need to tell you something else. Pajarito is making your mother's wedding dress."

Chapter 37

"No move, Rosaria." Pajarito tugged at the bottom of the long white dress for emphasis.

Rosaria opened her mouth to correct Pajarito's English and stopped. At least she was trying. "Dear friend, please take those pins out of your mouth when you talk. I fear you will choke on one. How much longer? I have so much to do."

"I sew dress. Daniela cook food. Eliazar fix house. We dress you. Lola make hair and face—how you say—beautiful. People come. You do nada."

"You make it sound so simple."

"Sí, is simple. No move." She stabbed at the air with a straight pin for emphasis.

Rosaria swallowed her rising anxiety and exhaled. She willed her restless body to quiet, straightened her spine, and planted her feet on the wooden kitchen table top. "There. I won't even breathe until you're finished."

Fabric rustled. She sensed Pajarito's position below her by the slight pull on her dress. Rosaria dared not move her head, but slid her eyes down to the cascades of white flowing to her feet. Pajarito must have used an entire bolt of material to fashion this creation.

Pajarito stood up. She took Rosaria's hand to help her down, from table top, to chair, to floor. "Come. See."

Rosaria followed Pajarito, steeling herself. Rosaria visualized a ceramic bride atop a cake, her billowing gown covering its entire top. A 23-year old would be stunning, but a 73-year-old? The dress swished as she walked. *I don't need to see. I know I look ridiculous. What will I say to Pajarito so I don't hurt her feelings?*

"See yourself."

Rosaria's first thought was that she looked taller, although it was an optical illusion. Embroidered red rose buds cascaded from her shoulders, down the bodice to her waist, creating a longer line and a slimmer middle. A scarlet sash circled her waist. The soft satin material clung to her body and draped in long gentle folds down to the tips of her shoes. Cinderella must have felt the same way after her transformation.

"Oh! It's beautiful. You are my fairy godmother," Rosaria said. "And you are my best friend."

"I make the dress white for the Virgin, and red flowers for you."

Alex opened his room door. "No dogs allowed."

"Diablo is allowed everywhere," Rosaria said.

Alex flung the door open and retreated into the room.

"He will not be a problem…unless you raise your voice to me. Sit. You, too, Alex."

Rosaria sat in the chair next to the bed, with Diablo

leaning against her leg. Alex sat on the edge of his mattress, wary eyes on Diablo. Rosaria nodded her head in approval when both man and dog had settled themselves.

"Alex, you will always be part of my life."

"What's your hurry? Why don't you take your time—think this through?"

"My hurry? At my age? How much time do I have?"

"Stop talking like that."

"It's the truth. I won't waste another moment of my life. I won't love you any less because I love Mario. I know you went through a terrible time, and I'm sorry. I wish I had done things differently."

"Doesn't change anything."

"Forgiving changes everything. You need to forgive me. I've forgiven you."

"Me? What did I do?"

"You cleaned out my house and sold it without one word until after it was done. I never would have believed you would do that to me."

"There was no way you could live there again. I took you to a place where you'd get good care."

"It no longer matters. Mario and I want to be together for whatever years we have left."

Alex ran his hand through his hair. "I can't—I won't—accept this." He stood up.

Diablo sprang to his feet, and a growl rumbled in his throat.

"Diablo, it's all right," Rosaria said.

Chapter 38

A few drinks in the cantina had done nothing to abate Alex's fury. As he climbed the stairs to his room, he marked each step with an internal mantra. *Damn you, Mom. Damn you, Mom.* She was choosing these strangers over him. He felt like he had lost her all over again. *Damn. Damn.*

"What's your hurry, amigo?" Cap said from behind Alex, each syllable punctuated with panting breaths.

Alex tried and failed to plunge the heavy key into his room lock. "Damn these old doors."

"Got to finesse it," Cap said. He took the key from Alex and eased it in. "See?"

He opened the door and stepped back. "Want some company?"

Alex shrugged. He wouldn't be able to clear his head anytime soon, so sleep was out of the question. If nothing else, Cap's chatter would make him drowsy, as it had during those long hours together on the road.

Cap poured two tall glasses of tequila from the bottle beside Alex's bed and gave one to Alex. He clinked his glass against Alex's. "To your mom. Her mind's sharp. She's healthy. And, for her age, she's a hottie."

"A hottie?" Alex body stiffened, and his face warmed.

"Mario thinks so."

"I appreciate your help, but I can take it from here. I'll arrange a ride for you to the nearest airport and pay for your ticket home. You can send me the bill for whatever else I owe you." Alex stood.

Cap didn't move. "Define 'take it from here.'"

"Her staying here isn't acceptable."

Cap upended his glass and swallowed the last inches of alcohol. With deliberate movements, he placed the glass on the nightstand. "What's not acceptable is you taking her back when she doesn't want to go. Look at her, really see her."

"Not your decision to make." Alex opened the door to the hallway. "Adiós."

Cap propped his sombrero against the chair and stood up. He folded his arms and stared at Alex. "Not leaving just yet. Not finished with our talk. Amigo, you're an a-hole."

"Thank you for that," Alex said. "Out."

"Who do you think you are? Your mother—in no way—wants to go back with you. And she's not going to change her mind in a few days, or ever. I don't know who she was before, but I see who she is now—a lady who has more balls than both of us put together."

"What am I supposed to do? Just let her go on here—until one day she falls, or has another stroke and can't take care of herself?"

"Exactly." Cap's index finger jabbed into Alex's chest with each word. "Let. Her. Go." The final jab pushed Alex back a step.

Alex shook his head. "I'm her son."

"Then act like one."

Alex threw his glass across the room to the wall, and it exploded.

"Feel better now?"

Alex formed his hands into hard fists as he stepped toward Cap. Before Alex could deliver a punch, Cap twisted his body away from Alex's punch. Alex found himself bent over in a tight choke hold, with his arms flailing. He felt Cap squeeze his neck in a viselike grip for several long moments. His vision began to blur, and his legs buckled. When his knees hit the floor, Cap let go. Alex clutched at his throat and gasped. He struggled to speak. "What do you think you're doing?"

"Getting your attention."

Alex sat back on his heels, his hands continuing to massage his throat. "You sure as hell got it."

Alex stretched out on his bed. He held a towel wrapped around ice chunks to his neck. Just like Cap to almost kill him and then bring him ice. Man, he was strong. *He could have finished me if he'd wanted, and the sheriff would be wrapping my entire body in ice.* His eyes smarted, and he wiped them with the edge of the towel. Grown men don't cry.

What had he expected? He thought he'd arrive and find a cowering, weak woman, joyous to be rescued by her son. Not this…. He covered his face with the towel. *Ah, Mom.*

Chapter 39

Alex found his seat, 13F. Unlucky 13. And add F for failure. He stared out the plane window into the blinding light. Why was this place so relentlessly sunny? Palms swayed in the breeze like a damn postcard.

Alex reached into his pocket and brought out his cell phone. He scrolled to the photo Cap took. His mother stood ram straight, a foot away. At Cap's command, she smiled a benign smile; Alex scowled. He had to admit she no longer resembled an old woman shrinking into the end of her life.

Someone sat down next to him. He closed his eyes and pretended to sleep.

Judith would be waiting for him. What was he going to tell her? The truth? A new concept in his marriage. Evasions and half truths had kept the peace. He would tell her everything from now on. The whole truth. He wanted to get home and repaint the small extra bedroom in baby shades of blue or pink. At 49, he knew he was a little old to become a dad; he had waited so long to marry. Judith was younger by 12 years, part of her allure. When they had talked about it—before they married—Judith wanted kids, too. Now he feared she had other ideas. She kept pool catalogues on her bedside table, and her birth control pills in the medicine cabinet. They never talked about much anymore, certainly not about babies, or pills, or pools. But, when he got home, they would talk, and plan their future. The baby first; the pool later, if she still wanted one. No reason they couldn't have both, he'd tell her.

More of the truth. His mother decided to stay behind. He was no longer the man in her life. She'd rather be with some Mexican farmer. What did she think she was doing—living in one of those Mexican romance novels she read? She wanted him to accept her decision to stay behind with those people, but he could not. Those people were foreigners to him. He felt 100 percent American. Well, she'd made her decision. Let her live with it. Judith and I will make our own family.

The plane bucked and bounced in air turbulence. Alex pulled his seatbelt tighter.

"Señor, por favor, ¿habla usted Espanol?"

"No. I do not speak Spanish." Alex continued to peer out the window.

"María, Madre de Dios."

He turned his head toward the voice. The wide, fearful eyes of an ancient woman met his. She clutched her rosary to the chest of her turquoise dress, which was embroidered with white crosses. Tears ran down her wrinkled cheeks and onto the neckline of her garment. Wearing her Sunday best. Probably her first flight. Lucky Row 13. Alex reached up to push the attendant call button. Before he could, an announcement crackled: "The captain has put on the seatbelt sign. Please stay in your seat with your seatbelt fastened."

His seat companion reached over and touched his arm. "Señor, ¿qué dijo?

"She told us to keep our seatbelts on and to stay in our seat," he replied in slow, careful English.

She shook her head and her hand flew to her mouth. "No comprendo."

Alex repeated his words in Spanish. "We will be fine," he added. "Watch the attendants." He pointed to the front of the cabin where two young women sat facing them. "See how calm they are. You have nothing to worry about."

The woman stretched her head out into the aisle to look at the attendants seated in the front. "Sí, la veo. Gracias, señor." She reached over, gave his arm a gentle pat, and settled back into her seat.

Ten minutes later, the seatbelt sign went off. Alex pointed to the darkened indicator and flipped open his seatbelt. "Take off your seatbelt. I will change seats with you. You can see out the window."

"You are most kind. Please, what name are you called?"

"Alex…Alejandro."

"I am called Socorro."

At the luggage carousel, he helped her retrieve her cardboard box tied with string and placed it on a luggage cart.

"Your mother is blessed to have such a son as you," she said.

She pushed the cart out through the automatic doors. Shouts broke out, and children and adults surrounded Socorro.

Judith waved to him from the car parked at the curb. The trunk was popped open for his luggage. He put his suitcase in and slid into the passenger seat. As he leaned in to her, she gave him a quick kiss, and pulled into the airport traffic.

"Who was that old lady with you? At first, I thought it was your mother," she said.

My mother is no longer an old lady like that.

"Someone I met on the flight," he said.

"No way someone that age should travel alone." Judith shook her head. "No way."

Your mother is blessed to have such a son as you. Is she?

"Why didn't your mother come with you? She too sick to travel?"

"She's fine."

"When's she coming back? How's that going to work? You can fly down to get her. Might be best to arrange for a wheelchair. She can't fly by herself."

"You'd be surprised what my mother can do."

"What's that supposed to mean?"

"Let's talk when we get home."

After weeks of dirt roads and pathways, Alex marveled at all the asphalt and concrete whipping past. The speed of everything unnerved him, beginning with the airport escalator that threw him and Socorro down into the baggage area. It had almost been her undoing; she clung to his arm and stumbled off at the bottom. Here on the freeway, cars and trucks roared on both sides of their car. Judith kept up with the flow of vehicles, her eyes straight ahead. He felt like he was in a wild race and not keeping up. His right hand gripped the arm rest. He closed his eyes to the chaos and leaned his head back against the headrest.

Alex felt the car slow and turn into their driveway. "The lawn looks great. Bushes are trimmed, too. You planted some colorful flowers. What're they called?"

"Not sure. The gardener picked them out."

"Who'd you hire? The guy the Hills use? He works good, long as they stay on him."

"I wanted someone I knew, someone I could trust. Hank needed the work."

"Not the bartender Hank?"

"Yes."

"You trust him? Wasn't he accused of pocketing money—back when you and I first met each other. They fired him, didn't they?"

"It was a mutual agreement."

"Bet it was."

"Hank wanted to move on to other opportunities. He's building up his landscaping business."

"I don't like the guy. He screwed his boss by stealing. He's planted his last flower on my property."

"You left me alone all this time to deal with everything. Then you come home and first thing you criticize me."

"I'll take care of my own yard."

"But it's a lot of work for you. Anyway, Hank has to work for the next six months—no charge."

"Why?"

"He's working off the money I…advanced him to buy his gardening tools."

"What the…? How much we talking about? You never said one word to me about him."

"Didn't want to bother you; you had enough to deal with. I bet you didn't tell me everything that went on down in Mexico with you and the fat guy, either. You only told me that you were coming home without him. He decided to stay on and enjoy some more Mexican girls? And why didn't you bring your mother along back with you? I told them at Shady Oaks she'd be back today. Did you at least bring back the money she took?"

"Let's have this conversation in the house."

The living room appeared the same, neat and tidy. As he passed the closed door of the extra bedroom, he opened it. How much paint would he need to transform it into the baby's room? He stood back. Instead of the original beige color, pale lavender adorned the walls. A bookcase stood against one wall, two dark leather lounge chairs faced a huge flat-screen television mounted on the opposite wall, and a small refrigerator hummed in a corner.

Alex moved to the window and pushed apart the frilly gauze curtains. A deep hole had been dug into the backyard grass. *A pool.* She had begun to build a pool. His hand bumped against something on the window ledge behind the curtain. A framed photo wobbled, and he reached down to right it before it fell. Judith, in a red bikini, stood holding a shovel plunged into the ground. Leaning against her, in matching red trunks, Hank held her in a tight embrace, his foot on the shovel. Both smiled broadly into the sun. A backhoe, its driver perched in the seat, waited behind the pair. He smiled, too.

Alex broke out in sweat. He gripped the curtains, and the rod broke away from the wall. Alex flung the tangle of curtains and rod across the room.

"Alex! What're you doing?" Judith stood in the doorway.

"I'm finished." The blood in his head continued its furious pumping. He took a deep breath and turned to her.

She backed away. She held up her hands, palms out. She ran to their bedroom, slammed the door, and the lock clicked into place.

The door broke away from its hinges on his first kick.

"Stay away from me." She touched her cell phone screen.

"No calls." Alex wrenched it from her hand. She stumbled backward onto the bed, scrambled away and sat against the headboard.

"You think you can screw around while I'm gone—that I'll come home, and never figure it out. That we'd take up right where we left off?"

"Alex, this isn't like you." She lowered her chin.

"Save that for Hank. I'm not interested." He stepped over the splintered door frame.

Chapter 40

Wedding plans swirled around Rosaria. Everything was happening so fast.

She had been so preoccupied with Alejandro, that she hadn't thought enough about Mario's daughters. Renata and Graciela. What would they have to say about a new woman in their father's life? Even though a decade had passed since their mother's death, Rosaria didn't expect them to welcome another female into the family. Mario spoke lovingly of his closeness to his "girls," to his grandchildren, to his sons-in-law, all of whom lived with him. She prayed their hearts would be more open than her son's had been.

And was Mario himself ready? He still carried his wedding photo in his wallet. "Her name was Fidelia. We were so young," he told Rosaria when he showed it to her.

Rosaria returned from the bathroom to find Mario pulling on his trousers.

"Today I will take you to see my home and meet my family," Mario said.

"Today?"

"Right after breakfast, we will go."

"Why must it be today?"

"Because I know you well, dear one. If I say tomorrow, you will find a reason to say no, as you have many times before. We go today, before you have time to worry yourself."

"Do your daughters know we're coming?"

"I may have mentioned it to them." He pulled her close and kissed her neck. "Now, get dressed, mi amor."

Mario sat tall in the truck, his hat tipped forward to block the sun. Dios, he was good looking. She continued to stare at him.

Mario glanced over at her. "What?

"Just thinking how lucky I am to be taking a ride with a handsome cowboy."

Mario tipped his head. "Gracias, mi amor."

After more than an hour of driving, he swung off the two-lane dirt road onto a one-lane that seemed like all the others they had passed.

"This is my driveway." He pointed out the windshield. A sturdy wooden gate blocked their way. He slowed, and it swung open for them to pass through.

"Transponder," Mario said. He indicated a decal on the windshield.

Even though the day was warm and cloudless, Rosaria felt chilled. She wrapped her shawl up around her shoulders, rubbed her hands together, and strained forward to watch for Mario's home. No dwellings anywhere. Low desert growth carpeted the ground. The earthen road disappeared into the horizon, a brown ribbon winding through a lonely landscape.

"How much of this is your land?"

Mario swept his hand from right to left. "All far as you can see. 20,000 hectares."

"I've thought in acres so long. That's 50,000 acres, isn't it?"

Mario nodded.

"How much farther?" Rosaria asked.

"You ask many questions, mujer. Another few minutes."

"I didn't know you traveled so far to see me."

"I do not mind."

Her apprehension grew during another ten minutes or more of driving. How could Mario and his family live so far from town and other people? Another wooden gate blocked their path. Just beyond it, a small wooden shed stood. Mario stopped. A man ran out of the structure to the gate and swung it open. Mario waved and accelerated through. Another man saluted them as they drove through the gate.

Rosaria swiveled around as the truck passed. "Those men have rifles."

"A precaution."

"Have you had problems?"

"Never."

"Then why the armed guards?"

"I keep my family safe."

Rosaria's skin prickled.

The truck traveled for more bumpy minutes along a

narrower road until a sprawling adobe structure came into view. Its tan color blended into the surrounding earth.

"Mi casa es su casa, Rosaria." He drove past tall desert willows that surrounded the perimeter of the home, providing a canopy of dappled shade. Deep pink blossoms adorned the graceful branches. Rosaria opened her window, and inhaled their sweet fragrance. The house spread out over the land with a vast foothold. A large porch with a shiny tile floor wrapped around the exterior. Groupings of wooden furniture filled the veranda. She could see into the center courtyard. At the back, a round water tower rose above the rooftop. She thought of Rapunzel. Two wings of the building extended out opposite directions and angled back toward the center.

"I had no idea. Your home is like a castle among the trees."

"I like that. When we marry, I will have a sign made for over our front door. *El Castillo entre los arboles de Mario y Rosaria.*"

Before Rosaria could form a response, children tumbled out the courtyard toward them. "¡Abuelo! ¡Abuelo! ¿Qué nos trajiste?"

Mario got out and reached behind the seat. He brought out a box, and held it up high. Two girls and three boys hopped in a dizzy circle around him.

"Abuelo, ¡dámelo!" a boy said.

"No, me!" the smallest girl danced with one hand out, the other on her hip.

A raven-haired young woman hurried out of the house

and called to the children. "¡Niños, dejen de gritar en este momento!" The children stopped and turned to her.

"Rosaria, come and meet my grandchildren," Mario said.

"Rosaria, this is Josefina." He reached into his box and handed the smallest child a little paper bag.

"Gracias, abuelo," she said.

"And what do you say to Señora Rosaria?"

"Estoy encantada—" Josefina said.

"English, please, little one," Mario said.

"I am pleased to meet you," Josefina said in a small voice.

"I am pleased to meet you, too, Josefina," Rosaria said. The child whirled and ran to the woman in the courtyard entryway.

Mario introduced each male grandchild in turn, from youngest to oldest: Jesús, Javier, and Jorge—each different sizes of dark-haired boys. How would she ever remember their names?

Mario put his arm around Rosaria's waist and led her to the porch. "Jesús got his name because he was the third boy born in a row. Graciela said with such a holy name, the Virgin Mother would allow her to stop giving birth to males. And she did. Josefina means 'God shall add another son.' My daughter has a blasphemous sense of humor."

"Father, you are terrible," the young woman said.

"Rosaria, this is my youngest daughter Graciela."

"Graciela, I am so pleased to meet you. Your father has told me much about you and his grandchildren." Rosaria smiled at Graciela, at Mario's handsome face in feminine form. On her, his strong jaw was softened. She would age well.

"I am pleased to meet you, too," Graciela said, but her dark eyes flashed something else.

"Where is Renata?" Mario asked.

A woman walked into the sun from the shade of the courtyard. Here, in the flesh, was the woman in Mario's wedding portrait. *How could he bear to see his eldest daughter every day and behold his dead wife?*

Rosaria pulled her shawl tight against her body.

Chapter 41

She closed her eyes. Her head ached. She wanted to get back home and crawl into bed, alone. Mario reached across the seat to caress her neck. "My angel," he whispered. She pretended to sleep and slumped against the passenger window, away from his proprietary touch. She loved him, but she was not his or anyone else's angel.

While she feigned sleep, she thought back over her afternoon at his home. His daughters had been coolly polite, taking her on a tour of the downstairs, with particular emphasis on the kitchen. Gleaming copper pots hanging from hooks; someone polished those. When she asked about a cook, the women had gaped at her, aghast. They were the cooks in this household. Rosaria said a fervent prayer of thanks for Daniela.

Mario had led her up a wide staircase to the second floor. Stern portraits lined the walls. Mario identified each as they passed, a blur of relationships and names. His people had been on this land for many years. He led her down a long hallway to the left of the stairs. To the right were his children's and grandchildren's rooms, he told her. We will have much privacy, he assured her.

He pushed open the heavy door. The room interior was darkened by heavy drapes hung over the two windows. He flicked a switch and an overhead fluorescent light sizzled to life. A double bed dwarfed by an imposing wooden headboard stood against the far wall. Add a statue of the Virgin Mary and some candles, and it could be a church altar. A tall wardrobe fulfilled the needs of a man's limited wardrobe, and a high chest of drawers occupied a far corner.

Rosaria moved closer to the bureau and saw on its top an enlarged version of the wedding photo Mario carried in his wallet. A lit voitive candle flickered light onto the smiling faces. A dozen or more statues of the Virgin Mary and Jesús completed the tableau.

In the far recesses of the room, a second wardrobe sat in the corner, a neat stack of women's hats and serapes atop it. A white cotton nightgown stuck out near the bottom of the closed doors. No end tables or lamps by the bedside to soften the harsh ceiling fixture, nor to allow reading in bed. Why had she assumed Mario was a reader?

The sons-in-law had lumbered into the dining room for lunch. Both were dark, muscular men, with slight pouches of belly above their heavy medal belt buckles. Felipe, Graciela's husband, stood almost a foot taller than Renata's husband Santiago. At least she would be able to tell them apart. The women clucked at them over their dirty boots, but the men kept them on. They threw their wide-brimmed hats onto a side table.

During lunch, Mario and his family passed pottery plates stacked with food around the dining table and chattered. She swiveled her head and tried to keep up with their rapid-fire Spanish. Mario attempted to lead the conversation back to her, and to remind them to speak English, but each speaker reverted to familiar Spanish after a few sentences. The men dominated the table with loud talk of fences and animals. The women spoke in soft voices to each other about recipes and children. These people took pride in the hard work they did each day and measured their days in tasks completed. She saw no place for herself here at this table—or in this house. The children ate with gusto, the J-named boys pausing only long enough to poke each other. This family was complete without her.

She felt the vehicle stop and sat up. Mario hurried around and opened her door. He offered his hand to help her step down.

He held her elbow as they walked to her porch steps. "What specialty do you suppose Daniela has prepared for our dinner?" he said.

"I am very tired and do not think I can eat. But, please, stay and eat. That will please Daniela and Pajarito." Rosaria kept her eyes on the path beneath her feet.

"I can wait while you rest—or rest with you—and eat later with you, mi mujer."

"No, eat now. I will probably not get up for dinner."

"Are you ill, mi amor?"

"No, I am only tired, very tired."

Did this man measure his life in meals eaten? Where had that unkind thought come from? For that matter, how did she measure her life? She was overly tired, never the time for reasoned thinking.

Mario pulled Rosaria into his embrace. She kept her head buried against his chest and did not raise her head for the kiss she knew he was waiting to give her. She felt him watching her as she walked to her bedroom. The late afternoon sunlight streamed across her room. She pushed the white cotton curtains open wide, and fell onto her bed. Warm air drifted over her, and she closed her eyes. She heard Mario's voice, laughter, and then nothing.

She needed the bathroom. What time could it be? Moonlight lit the room and cast shadows. She crept down the hallway to the toilet. On her return to her bed, she tiptoed into the living room. The sofa was empty. For the first time, her heart leapt at his absence, rather than his presence.

Chapter 42

"Turn around and go back there." Cap's voice on the cell phone sounded loud and close. Alex half hoped to see Cap on the bench seat next to him.

"Can't do that."

"You can and you will. Unless you want Judith to claim you deserted her, ran off to Mexico. You do, and she gets everything."

"I don't care."

"You're mad as hell and not thinking straight. Go back. Don't move out. Keep your cool. I'll give you the name of a lawyer. He'll tell you the same thing. Do it."

Alex drove around and around the block, passing his house again and again, until he felt his breathing slow. *I can do this.* He parked in his usual spot in the driveway.

When he opened the front door, a vacuum cleaner whirled from the back of the house.

"Honey, I'm home," Alex sang under his breath. He snorted at his own private joke. He walked down the hall toward the noise, and pulled the cord out of the outlet as he passed.

Judith's perplexed face appeared in the den doorway. "Hank?" Her face lit, first with surprise, then with anger.

"Get out of here," she said.

"No. I'll be staying. And don't worry. I won't touch you."

"Hank'll be here any minute."

"Call him and tell him now's not a good time."

Alex plugged the vacuum in, and it roared back to life.

He woke with a headache and a sore neck. The living room sofa was more decorative than comfortable, and certainly not intended for a good night's sleep. Still, he preferred it to sharing Judith's bed. Her bed. No longer theirs.

From the bathroom, he heard Judith clattering around in the kitchen. By the time he opened the door, he smelled coffee and pancakes. Judith sat at the kitchen table with her back to him. The small television on the counter filled the room with strident female voices, arguing the benefits of Botox.

She plunked a cup of coffee in front of Alex, and coffee sloshed over its rim. "I made blueberry pancakes from your mother's recipe." She bent low to put a plate of them down. Her plump breasts protruded from a low-cut nightgown. *Ah, Judith. You don't give up.*

Judith turned off the television. "What's going on with your mother?"

"Why does it matter to you? You never even liked her. What's going on with Hank?"

He felt her body lean against his arm. She bent down, and her breath tickled his ear. Despite himself, he felt his body stir. "Nothing's going on with Hank. I just hired him to do some yardwork. You're tired and over-reacting. Right now, you need to deal with you mother. She needs to be brought home. You need to go back down there and stop this nonsense. We have too much at stake."

"We? There's no we anymore, Judith."

Cap's name was gone from the door—replaced by *Atomic Exterminators*, painted in bright red letters. Atomic? Like they blasted bugs with hydrogen bombs? Alex couldn't wait to call Cap and tell him. He'd have a quick retort and a good laugh. *God, I miss that guy.*

Andrew Fortnoy, Attorney at Law, occupied a corner office on the same floor. The clean-faced young man's too-neat desk and lack of secretarial assistance didn't trouble Alex. The young attorney would be hungry for business and eager to prove himself, and to pay his rent.

"It's great that you're divorcing after only four years," the young man said as he pumped Alex's hand. He drew back his hand and flushed. "That didn't come out right. I meant your divorce will be simple because it's only been four years. At ten years, your wife would be entitled to half your assets."

"My only assets are my house and my business. I'm a one-person operation. I contract out for my workers."

"Let me see your business license." He studied it, flipped it onto the copier, and pushed a button. "You started this business before your marriage?"

Alex nodded.

"She can't claim any of it. How about the deed to your house?"

Alex handed it over. "It's paid off. I know she'll want to keep it, but she can't afford to buy me out. I want to sell it to someone, and give her whatever money..."

Fortnoy examined the document. "How does the number zero sound to you?"

Alex punched his cell phone with more pressure than necessary.

"The asshole Hank's parked in my driveway," Alex said into the phone.

"Easy, amigo. Don't mess with this guy. Put it in reverse. Get yourself a coffee," Cap said.

"He's not keeping me out of my own house."

"Alex, calm down."

"I'm calm."

"You don't sound like it. You beat him up, you think you'll feel better. But all it'll get you is a domestic abuse accusation. She'll be on the phone to the cops. Hell, that woman might punch herself in the face to get back at you. Stay away."

"I'm not hitting anyone."

Alex slammed the truck door shut with a loud bang that he hoped announced his arrival. He put his key in the front lock. It wouldn't go in. *Damnit!* He rang the door bell and knocked.

The door cracked open, and Hank's face appeared above the chain. "You threatened Judith. Go away, or we call the cops on you." He tried to close the door, but Alex leaned into it.

"Please call them, or I will."

Judith's face appeared. Alex held up the paper.

"My mother and I own this house. You and your friend are trespassing."

Chapter 43

She avoided being alone with Mario the following week. Pajarito and Daniela noticed and cast worried glances her way, but she pretended not to notice.

Rosaria gazed at her gown, her wedding gown, hanging on a hook in Pajarito's bedroom across the hall. Pajarito insisted on keeping it there for her finishing touches. If the wedding didn't occur soon, the fabric would disappear under embroidery and sequins. The windows were closed to the afternoon heat. Rosaria shut her eyes and sensed the benign ghosts of her parents in their old bedroom.

Mamá, what should I do? At that moment, her wedding dress slipped off one side of the hanger and dangled askew. *Mamá.* Rosaria picked up and rehung the dress. She recoiled from its cold satin smoothness.

Rosaria knew what she had to do. She was having second thoughts. Not merely second thoughts. Her second thoughts led to third thoughts, and back to her first thoughts, a circle of doubts. Although his daughters had been formally polite to her, they had not displayed a trace of warmth. Their unspoken words were loud: *You are a guest in our home with our father, and nothing more.* She had left there shaken by their aloofness.

And it wasn't just them; it was the ranch itself. She felt disquieted by its isolation. The wind blew, unimpeded, across his land from the far horizon, and buffeted the trees surrounding his hill-top compound. So far from town, from her home, from her friends, especially dear Pajarito. Pajarito depended on her. And her parents still comforted to her with their presence in their casa. *How can I abandon the living and the dead?*

She tried to imagine what a day would be like for her out there. She could only read so many books to herself, and she couldn't fathom his daughters being still long enough to hear her read aloud to them. They had their daily tasks and would want her to stay out of their way. She could read to the children, but they would be occupied with their home studies. And, of course, the men had their outdoor work. She'd be lucky to see Mario before dinner time, and then at a table full of his bustling family. *Was their life together to be confined to that dark bedroom?*

Every bride must question her choice, she reasoned. No, she remembered plunging into her marriage to Longino without a doubt. But she had been so young. She was a different woman now, a half century older. She reached out to touch the gown again.

"Rosita! No touch!" Pajarito swatted the air for emphasis and advanced. "Go."

"Pajarito…"

"Go."

Rosaria twisted her braids into place and pushed bobby pins through them. "Good enough," she announced to herself.

Diablo bumped her hand.

"Let's go for a walk, good boy."

Beyond the promenade, a few people sat on the narrow beach. Rosaria led Diablo across to the wet sand just above the water's edge. She breathed in the salty air, and the incoming breeze cooled her face. Sporadic incoming ripples of water slapped at their feet. Diablo high stepped as though he didn't want to get his paws wet, but Rosaria knew better. If she removed his leash, he would make a mad dash into the water. Despite countless futile attempts, he still believed he could catch the sea birds floating on the water.

"Diablo, I love Mario. You know I do. He's a good man."

So, what's the problem?

"Problems really. His daughters resent me, and..."

Like your son resents him?

"Don't change the subject. Plus, Mario lives way out in the desert."

So?

"I like living near the village. I can't see myself stuck out there. Here, I have the company of my friends, and people come to hear me read to them. Plus, I have Pajarito to think of."

She has her son.

"But I promised her a home with me."

Have you asked her what she wants?

"She wants to stay with me."

Her son is adding rooms to his home. Maybe Pajarito

would prefer to live with him and her future grandchildren.
Perhaps she is afraid of hurting your feelings by telling you this.

Rosaria stopped and put her hands on her hips. "Oh…I
never thought of it that way."

And the bigger question is: what do you want?

When had Diablo's voice in her head morphed into her
mother's?

"Mamá?" she said.

She unsnapped his leash and watched Diablo bolt into
the water.

Rosaria sat on the porch reading aloud from a new book,
practicing for today's audience. From the interior, Pajarito's
sewing machine whirred like busy insects humming a daytime song. Pajarito had dug this particular book out of her
boxes she kept from her selling days, demanding that Rosaria
read it next. "Amor Triunfa Sobre Todo." *Love Triumphs Over*
All. Fiction for sure.

"Is very, very good," Pajarito had said. She tapped the
cover. A man with flowing dark hair held a woman against
his bare chest with one muscular arm. In the other, he brandished a sword. In the background, a mansion burned. The
young woman's terrified yet adoring face gazed up at him.
She was the standard young damsel in distress, her dress torn
in strategic places to expose most of her breasts and thighs.
Was she afraid of her circumstances, or of him? Probably
both. Yet another strong man to save a weak woman.

Three pages in, Rosaria had read enough sex and violence to know Pajarito was right. The men would protest at the title, but get caught up in the story despite themselves; and the women would adore both the title and the book.

She practiced the projection of her voice she would need later. The men who stood in the back must be able to hear her. "I cannot give myself to you! I am betrothed to another!" Her voice cracked with emotion.

"Who is he? I will kill him!" a familiar male voice said.

The garden gate swung shut. Mario strode up the steps.

"Tell me his name, and I will dispatch him to hell!" Mario swooped his hat off his head and took her right hand. He kissed it and held it. "Speak, fair señora. Speak."

"Mario...I...," The words disappeared as her decision came to her. She hadn't come to the decision; it had come to her. Rosaria dissolved into tears.

"What is the matter?" Mario said. He kneeled in front of her. "What has happened?"

"I love you so much, but.... Your daughters want your lives to remain the same. They do not want another woman coming into the home you shared with their mother." She raised her hand to forestall any protest from him. "And I must tell you, too, that I'm not sure I can leave my own life here. Pajarito is my responsibility; I have promised to take care of her. I can't bear the thought of leaving my childhood home. I have created my own little paradise, right here. Can you understand?"

"My daughters will treat you with respect. If they do not, I will not tolerate it." He stood up and began to pace to the edge of the porch and back to her.

"You talk about them as though they're still children. They have been polite to me. But it is too much to expect them to welcome me into their lives."

"They will welcome you. I will see to that."

Rosaria shook her head. "You cannot force them to accept me."

"In my house, my word is law." He set his hat back on his head. "They will obey me."

Rosaria sat up straight, and her hands tightened on the arms of her chair. "And in your home, am I to obey you, too?"

"I did not say that. It will be our home."

"Your home is already full of people. Where would I fit in? What would be my purpose?"

"Purpose? You will be my wife!"

"And move into your bedroom, that shrine to your dead wife?" Rosaria put her hand to her mouth. His face showed her that she had gone too far.

Mario spoke quietly. "I have offered to take you into my family. Your son has treated you with disrespect and left you alone. Who knows if you'll ever see him again?"

"That's a cruel thing to say to me."

"It is true. No?"

"Alejandro and I will work out our differences."

"Why can't you see what your life with me would be like? Why do you have to be so stubborn?"

"I see it—very clearly. I cannot be the woman you expect. We would end up unhappy with each other."

"You're too American...so determined to be...*independent*." He said the word like an obscenity.

How long had he thought that?

"Yes, I am. Independent." She stood up and stared straight into his eyes.

Mario nodded his head once, like he acknowledged the truth of her words. "I'll be going."

"Yes," she said.

He opened the gate and paused. Rosaria clasped her hands together. *He will turn around and come back.* Mario stood in place more seconds, then stepped outside her yard.

"Here's my own beautiful dress." Pajarito lifted the bright crimson garment. "Like roses on your gown."

"Oh, Pajarito." Rosaria brought her handkerchief to her face. "Pajarito, are you happy here…living with me?"

"I love living with you." She studied Rosaria's face. "You are worried about what will happen to me after you marry."

"I'm sorry, dear friend. I've been so selfish, thinking only of myself."

"No worry. Julio promise. Build room for me. He marry one day, and I help with babies. I pray for many."

"Are you certain this is what you want?"

"Sí, sí, mi amiga." Pajarito turned back to her sewing.

Rosaria paused in the doorway. "Pajarito, please tell the people I am sorry. I will not be reading to them today."

"What is wrong?"

"I am tired. I will feel better after a nap."

"You sure?'

I'm sure of nothing. "Yes, I need to sleep."

Rosaria placed her hand on Diablo's head and kept it there as they walked to her bedroom. He circled his mat and lay down. She settled on top of the bedspread and put her hand on her heart

For a week, Pajarito and Daniela persisted. "Where is Mario? Is he not well?"

After the third week, their questions stopped, although Rosaria found them whispering like co-conspirators. The wedding was four Saturdays from now. She needed to cancel the arrangements, but she felt paralyzed. She did not want to admit that all hope was dead. Despite Mario's lack of communication, she kept expecting him to come to her. To apologize. To say that's why he loved her, for her independence. To say he couldn't live without her. To say let's live happily ever after—together—anywhere, just so we're together.

I've read too many romance novels.

"Rosaria, you must eat," Daniela said. She stood over Rosaria at the breakfast table.

"Eat, or wedding dress too big for you," Pajarito said.

The smell of the food repulsed her. She felt the eyes of Pajarito and Daniela on her.

"Rosaria, if you will not eat, we will bring the doctor," Daniela said.

"I will drink this juice and tea. Daniela, can make me a poached egg and a piece of toast, please?"

Rosaria sat on the porch, rocked, and stared out at her garden. Diablo slept in the far corner in the shadow of the flowering vines. He had given up trying to persuade her to take him on walks. For the last several weeks, Rosaria opened the garden gate and let him run out, calling him to return after a few minutes of freedom.

Pervasive sadness muted the brilliant flowers and the melodious songs of the birds. She pulled her robe around her. Getting out of her night clothes, bathing, and dressing confounded her. What a mess she'd made of things. She hadn't meant to hurt Alejandro or Mario. But both men wanted to define and confine her. To Alejandro, she was an old woman who required supervision in a facility. To Mario, she was a replacement wife who would slide into his life in an isolated fortress. She was neither.

The chatter of women reached the porch. Four women advanced toward the house, with Eliazar in the lead.

Chapter 44

She hoped Eliazar and her female posse hadn't spotted her on the porch. Rosaria rose from her chair, pulled her robe closed, and crept toward the front door.

"Wait, Rosaria!" Eliazar said.

Rosaria's hand flew to her face, and she turned around to face them. "Oh. I was not expecting anyone."

"I can see that." She studied Rosaria. "Rosaria, you are a mess."

"Thank you, it's good to see you, too."

"A friend tells a friend the truth."

"I'm not feeling well. Perhaps you could come back another day."

"We are here now." Eliazar swept her arms out, palms up. The three women behind her smiled weakly. Rosaria recognized them, one of Eliazar's daughters and two daughters-in-law.

"Girls, follow me," Eliazar said. She stepped up onto the porch, and the women followed in single file.

Rosaria stood blocking the door. Diablo rumbled deep-throated warnings. "Let's talk on the porch. My dog is not friendly."

"Your dog will not bother us." Eliazar reached into her huge straw purse and pulled out a large raw-hide bone.

Rosaria opened the door. Diablo confronted Eliazar, sniffed the bone she held out, and took it between his big jaws. He settled into a corner of the porch with it.

"Sí, that is a ferocious beast you have," Eliazar said. She swept past Rosaria. "Whew, Rosaria." She pinched her nose shut. "How long since you bathed? Never mind. Do not answer. We are here to clean you up."

"Now wait a minute. You're not all...."

"No, just me. Girls, go to the kitchen and talk with Daniela. I'll call you when I need you. Rosaria, you march to the bathroom. No more talk."

Rosaria walked down the hall like a condemned prisoner facing humiliation by washing.

Eliazar filled the rub with hot water, too hot until Rosaria mixed in some cold. Rosaria hiked up her nightgown and stepped into the oval tub. She drew the gown over her head, sat low in the water, and covered her breasts with her arms. The warm liquid enveloped her body, and she felt her muscles begin to relax...until Eliazar began to scrub her back with a coarse cloth.

"Ouch. Not so hard!"

"Your arms are like little sticks." Eliazar held up her own hefty arm. "See. This is the arm of a woman!"

Rosaria sank deeper into the water.

"I wash your hair, too." Eliazar pushed Rosaria's head down. Rosaria slid beneath the surface, and fought against the pressure of Eliazar's hand.

"You're drowning me!"

"Stop complaining."

Eliazar's poured shampoo onto Rosaria's head and kneaded Rosaria's scalp. A pleasant calm crept over Rosaria, interrupted by Eliazar's command, "Rinse!" She tipped Rosaria's head back and poured water from a basin.

Eliazar wrapped a towel around Rosaria's head and held out another. She opened the bathroom door, and called into the hallway, "Girls, we're ready!" Strong arms, strong voice. "Into your bedroom, Señora Rosaria."

"I do not need anyone's help."

"Rosaria, move." Eliazar's hands pushed into Rosaria's back.

One young woman held underwear and a cotton half-slip in her finger tips. Another cradled a floral-patterned dress that Rosaria recognized as one she hadn't worn in a long time. From her purse, Eliazar's daughter brought out an array of cosmetics and spread them across Rosaria's dressing table.

"Where is her bra?" Eliazar asked.

"I do not wear a bra."

"No need for it…for you." Eliazar stood straighter and pushed out her chest.

"And, I do not wear that fancy dress around my house."

"You wear it today. You never know when you'll have visitors stop by…maybe a special visitor."

The younger women smiled broadly.

"If you're talking about Mario, he won't be coming by. But I'm sure you know all about that."

"Me? I know nothing…nothing at all. Get dressed."

"I need privacy, please," Rosaria said. Water dripped down her body onto the wooden floor.

Eliazar grabbed the undergarments and dress and pushed them into Rosaria's hands. "Here. We will talk more to Daniela. Come, girls." She paused in the doorway and turned around. "Wear the dress I chose."

Rosaria toweled her body dry and lowered the colorful frock over her head. She examined herself. The dress hung shapelessly on her curveless body. She cinched the fabric belt tight around her waist. Rosaria spied the vanity table surface covered with brushes, combs, hair pins, and makeup. *I'm in for it.* She walked over to the bedroom window, opened it, and looked down. As a child, she had leaped down with ease and escaped to cavort in the night-time garden. Her leaping and cavorting days were over. Too bad.

Within minutes, Eliazar and her minions reappeared. "Better," she said. "Sit. Your wedding is in four weeks. Today we will practice on your hair style and makeup."

Eliazar's eyes glared. *Contradict me at your peril,* they said. "We have talked with Daniela and the menu for the reception is set. My daughter will make the decorations. She is very artistic." Her daughter's crimson cheeks and lips appeared in the reflection next to Eliazar.

"I'm not getting married."

"Don't be silly. Every bride gets nervous."

"You aren't listening to me. I have decided…"

"Be quiet and be still, Rosaria. We have work to do," Eliazar said.

Rosaria gave herself up to the ministrations of the women.

Finally, the women were gone. Rosaia stepped off the porch and out her gate. After weeks of inactivity, her legs would ache tomorrow. Diablo ran ahead of her on the path and leaped off it to disappear for minutes at a time. She could hear him crashing around and smiled at his pleasure. After half an hour, she called him, and he trotted to her side. He put his head against her hand. She stroked his head.

"Good boy. We will walk again tomorrow."

At the word "walk," his ears stood up. He deserved more from her than she had been giving. "I promise, dear Diablo."

From a distance, Rosaria saw a man sitting on her porch. Her heart jumped. It would be just like Eliazar to clean Rosaria up and then summons Mario. She could be so bossy. Well, at least I'm presentable. If he had seen me before.

"Diablo, how's the big boy?" Cap's booming voice reached Rosaria's ears before her eyes could identify his face.

Rosaria huffed up the steps. "Cap, how are you?"

He grabbed her into a bear hug. "Hello, beautiful señora. You all right? You're breathing kind of hard."

"Wait until you're my age. I need to sit down. Will you ask Daniela for some water for me and for Diablo, please? Get something for yourself, too. I know you're here to see her anyway."

"Already did. Be back in a minute for a sit-down with you, my number one señora."

Rosaria lifted her eyebrows.

"Daniela's my number one señorita."

Rosaria and Cap settled into companionable rocking. His big frame protruded out the sides of the rocker. If he stood up too quickly, he'd bring the chair with him, attached to his rear-end. She laughed quietly at the image.

"Good to hear you laugh, señora. It's been awhile."

"I haven't felt like laughing for awhile."

He locked his gaze on the garden. "We got together and talked, and we…decided that…."

"Who's *we*?"

"Your friends, señora…Pajarito, Daniela, Eliazar. They only want what is best for you."

"That's what Alex and Judith said…right before they put me away and sold my house. No one—no one—will ever again decide 'what's best for me.'" She stood over him, her hands on her hips.

"Darn it. I told them I wasn't the one to talk to you. 'Cap, you go,' Pajarito said. 'You can always make her laugh.' How about I toss in a knock-knock joke right about here?"

Rosaria tried not to smile and failed. "Cap, you're crazy."

"And proud of it." He reached over to her and took her hand. "We've been really worried about you, Señora Rosaria. You look a lot better now that you're cleaned up. Sorry, that didn't come out right. You know what I mean."

Rosaria grinned. "You have a way with words."

"Made you smile again." He commenced rocking. "You scared us."

Rosaria patted his hand. "I'm glad you decided to stay in Flores Bonitas, Cap. I don't miss Alejandro quite as much when you're around."

"I called Alex yesterday. Says he'll fly down for the wedding."

"There's not going to be a wedding. Tell him to save his money. That should thrill him and Judith. Especially Judith."

"Ah…there is no more Judith."

Rosaria's head shot up. "What?"

"She took up with some guy. Hey, I think Alex needs to tell you this. Not my place. And what's this about no wedding? I drove out to see Mario the other day."

"That your group's idea, too?"

He stopped rocking. "Please, Rosaria, this is hard enough for me."

"I'm sorry. How is he?"

"Why don't you ask him yourself?" He nodded his head toward the yard. The gate swung open.

Chapter 45

Cap stood over Rosaria. "Stay right where you are. Don't make me get physical with you, little lady." He pointed a meaty finger in her direction.

She shook her head at him. "This you and your committee's idea?"

"You betcha." He tipped his hat at her. "I'm going in to talk to Daniela now. But I'll listen for any raised voices out here."

"Yes, Mother," Rosaria said.

"Hi there, Mario. Good to see you," Cap said.

He and Mario shook hands as Mario ascended the porch steps. Cap turned, pointed two fingers from his eyes to Rosaria's, and went inside. As he did, Diablo ran out the door past him. The dog woofed a greeting and ran circles around Mario.

"Easy, Diablo," Mario said. He thumped the dog's back. "And are you happy to see me, too, Rosaria?"

Rosaria kept her head down and her eyes on Mario's pointed boots.

"How are you?" he asked. He bent over her and touched her shoulder.

"I am well. And you?"

"I would be better if you would look at me."

She studied his face, and saw no hint of anguish. *Just like a man. Life goes on.* He'd probably already found a new dance partner at the cantina—not that she cared. And he hadn't missed many meals grieving—more belly than she remembered. An image of him in her bed flashed into her mind. Her face flushed.

"You have good color, Rosaria," Mario said. "May I sit with you? I have missed you. I am sorry that I spoke harsh words to you."

"You said what you meant."

"I have decided…"

"You decided? No input from the intervention committee?"

"I do not understand. What committee?"

"People around here who have decided they know what is best for me."

"I know nothing of this. I am here to tell you…"

"To tell me what your plan is for me."

"I have a plan…for us."

Rosaria stood. "I am very tired. I usually nap at this time."

"Wait. I have come all this way to speak to you. Stay out here with me."

"Please excuse me."

"I will wait."

Rosaria peeked at him from the house. Mario tipped his hat down over his face, and leaned back in the rocker. His long legs stretched out until his boots touched the banister. He wasn't going anywhere anytime soon. Diablo curled into a companionable ball against his feet.

Rosaria couldn't find a comfortable position on her bed. Her brain wouldn't quiet, and her eyes kept popping open. Perhaps if she stared at the ceiling, fatigue would overtake her. It didn't. After half an hour, she gave up.

She heard Mario's soft snores through the closed front door. Rosaria carried a pitcher of water and a glass to the porch. As she settled into her rocker, Diablo lumbered to his feet, shaking his body as he did. His identification tag rattled against his collar.

Mario pushed back his hat and wiped at his face. "I thought it was a bad idea to come over, unannounced. Cap said if I asked you, you would say no, but that you would really mean yes. He said he had a lot more experience with women." Mario took a drink of water.

"Nothing's changed," Rosaria said.

"Come. Let's take a walk."

Rosaria strolled beside Mario on the foot path—two companions taking a walk, that's all.

Golden late afternoon light wafted through the palms overhead, and the fronds glistened in the gentle breeze. *My favorite time of day, my happy hour. Like God has gilded His world in gold.*

Diablo bounded ahead on the familiar path to the sea. Within sight of the ocean, Mario called Diablo back and led them off on a narrower path to the left. Mario quickened his pace, and Rosaria struggled to keep up. He stopped abruptly and pointed.

"From that palm to that." he gestured. "I have bought it. Here, we will build our house."

Rosaria swiveled. "Oh," she said.

"I will build whatever house you wish for us. I do not care, only that you are in it, with me."

"My house is close by. Why build another?"

"We will need something bigger, for our families when they visit. Your house is yours, and my house is mine. What we build will be ours. And behold the view we will have." He gestured toward the sun-capped sea.

"What about your ranch and all your work out there?"

"My daughters' husbands can handle it. They'll be glad I'm out of the way. They've done most of the work lately. I'll sign the deed over to them and my daughters."

"Mario, this is so much for me to absorb."

"Cap said it would be—that I should give you time to think it over."

"Cap? Who else have you told?"

"Only Cap. I swore him to secrecy."

The entire village knows.

On the way back, Rosaria crooked her arm through Mario's. Physical contact with him comforted her. He had apologized, offered to build her a house—yet nothing felt resolved—not yet.

Mario left after dinner, leaving Rosaria to sort through her emotions. She retreated to her bedroom, and sat at her desk. Writing in her notebook often helped her clarify her thinking and calmed her whirling mind. Rosaria began to write a list.

I must tell Mario:

1. I will maintain my financial independence.

2. My parents' casa will remain mine, and Pajarito may stay in my casa so long as she wishes.

3. I will continue to reach out, with love, to Alejandro.

She felt the knot in her stomach relax. She pulled a fresh sheet of paper from her desk drawer.

Dearest Mario,

She turned on the table lamp and wrote until the sun drifted below the trees. She sat back in her chair and re-read what she had written. She especially liked the last page.

God saved my best gift for the last of my life—you, dearest Mario.

I will enter our marriage as your partner. To do that, I will pay for half of the beautiful lot you have selected, and my share of our new home's construction.

And I will live the rest of my life by your side in our new casa by the sea. Casa Junto Al Mar! We will sit, on our front porch (There will be one, right?), look out at the waves, and marvel at our blessed time together.

I hope I have not overwhelmed you with my letter, but I must speak what is in my heart. Know that I love you, now, and forever.

Rosaria

Chapter 46

Happy the bride the sun shines on today. Or not. Monsoon rain rattled on the roof, and ran down the rainspouts. Rosaria shrugged at God's perverse sense of humor. No dark skies would dampen her joyous mood today. She sang to Pajarito at the breakfast table: "Here comes the bride…"

Father Antonio arrived at the church, a dark vision in the darker gloom, sheltered under his large black umbrella. "Hola, Rosaria. Wet enough for you?" He shook the excess moisture off his umbrella and folded it.

"Good thing you're a holy man, or I'd have some choice words for you. Here's a towel."

She handed him one from the stack Daniela had brought.

Behind Father Antonio, groups of early arrivals, determined to get good seats, hurried up the pathway to escape the the storm. Eliazar and her family emerged from the pack. "Come, come, Rosaria." Eliazar grabbed her arm and pulled her through the sanctuary to the choir room, today their dressing room.

"Get out of that robe," Eliazar said. Pajarito carried Rosaria's wedding dress to her and gently lowered it over her head. Dress in place, Eliazar laid a big towel over her shoulders to protect the fabric. Lola approached with her makeup magic and went to work.

"Gorgeous. Now, comb out her hair and re-braid it. Here are the ribbons to braid into it. Make it really tight…no stray hairs flying out." Eliazar held up one fist full of white ribbons, the other full of red ones.

Rosaria braced herself for pain and closed her eyes. She dare not get teary and ruin her makeup. Eliazar and Lola would not stand for that.

Plus, if she began to cry, she might never stop. A month ago, when Rojo was to drive Alex to Loreto International Airport, she had dressed and waited in her home, but her son had not come to say goodbye. How could he be so cruel, especially when their bond had been so strong? Perhaps she had spoiled him, to make up for his fatherless childhood, made him feel entitled. But, in retrospect, she would not have changed one moment of their lives together. When Rojo returned in Alex's truck, alone—so proud of his first vehicle— Rosaria locked herself in her bedroom for the afternoon.

Today she would not think about Alex. He told Cap he was coming, and he wasn't here. Their relationship would mend another day. She would keep trying. She willed her mind away from Alex to today and onto more pleasant thoughts. Mario's face. Mario's naked body. She smiled.

"See. You're not hurting her, Lola. She's enjoying herself," Eliazar said.

Cap led Rosaria from the choir room, down the corridor, around a pillar to the back of the church. She gasped. Every pew was filled. People sat shoulder to shoulder. The overflow stood ringing the hall.

Strains of the wedding march began and swelled until the music was loud enough to rattle the windows. People covered their ears. Rojo, volunteer DJ, mouthed sorry to the assembly and hurried to the ovesiízed cassette player. He rewound the tape, and the march screeched a hasty retreat. With a click, he restarted the tape, adjusting it from a blast to a comfortable listening level. Rojo caught Rosaria's eye. He gestured for her to come forward and increased the volume of his music again. As he did, her friends turned around to face her.

She slipped her right hand through Cap's arm. He laid his left hand atop hers and squeezed. To everyone's surprise, Cap had outfitted himself in tasteful attire, black slacks and a white guayabera embellished with red trim. Closer inspection revealed the trim to be small chili peppers. Cap had explained his choice. He could wear this shirt again and again, perhaps for his own wedding.

"You sure you want that guy, and not me? Last chance." Cap said.

Mario stood at the front of the church, ram straight, his dark eyes locked on her like she was the only one in the room. Beside him, El Commandante nudged him, and jostled the single red rose bud pinned to Mario's white cotton western shirt. Mario's eyes never left Rosaria. His graying hair was slicked back, the curly ends slipping over his collar. Rosaria had rarely seen him without his straw hat on his head or in his hands. He clasped his empty hands in front of himself.

She elbowed Cap. "Behave yourself." Rosaria sensed someone behind her and turned her head. Alex. He tapped Cap on the shoulder.

"I believe this is my dance," Alex said.

"Sure thing, amigo," Cap replied.

Rosaria transferred her trembling arm to her son's. Alex stepped into place and squeezed her hand.

"Thank you, Alejandro."

"Mom. Don't you start crying."

Cap brought Diablo to Rosaria's left side and handed her his leash. Red and white ribbons wound around her loyal companion's collar, with a white satin pillow fastened atop his neck. Nestled within the pillow, their silver wedding rings glistened, secured by a red bow.

"Really, Mom? That dog has to be here?"

"Yes, he does. Be a good boy, Alejandro."

Rojo gestured an impatient *come, come,* with both arms.

Rosaria, Alejandro, and Diablo stepped forward.

Acknowledgments

Rosie Sees the Light would not have seen the light of day without Adrianne Fincham Quiros. She insisted my short story *had* to become a novel, and she assisted me throughout the long writing process. Without Adrianne's generous critiques and enthusiastic cheerleading, I would have given up. ¡Muchas gracias, mi amiga!

Sincere appreciation to Mary Rakow, my editor, whose expertise created order out of chaos. She treated me and my novel respectfully and professionally throughout our editing collaboration.

¡Muchas gracias! to Melanie Ashen, for checking and correcting my Spanish.

Thank you, too, to the Witty Women Writers, my eagle-eyed critique group: Cathryn Andresen, Kathleen Auth, Pat Caloia, Sheli Ellsworth, Bonnie Goldenberg, Lee Wade, and Claudette Young. We've shared some incredible writing and some delicious potluck dishes during our afternoons together.

More thanks to Sheli Ellsworth, whose final proofreading polished my book, and gave me the confidence to send Rosie into the world.

Gratitude and love to Connie Highberg, cherished friend, who was the first reader of my finalized novel.

Jose Ramirez of Pedernales Publishing LLC. deserves my deepest gratitude. His professionalism and commitment to excellence produced a book interior and cover of highest quality.

Finally, gratitude to my husband, Ronald, who learned that a closed den door meant I was off with Rosie on another adventure.